Mysteryville

Mysteryville

by
Jules Lermina

translated, annotated and introduced by
Brian Stableford

A Black Coat Press Book

Table of Contents

Introduction

"Mystère-Ville," here translated as "Mysteryville," was first published as a seventeen-part serial in the *Journal des Voyages*, running from December 4 1904 to March 26 1905, under the pseudonym of William Cobb. It was not reprinted in book form until 1998, when the small press Apex issued an edition of 250 copies. It is, however, the best of all Jules Lermina's works of fiction; the fact that he issued it under a pseudonym and did not manage to get it reprinted as a book presumably reflects the sensitivity of its subject-matter. Although it appeared in the *Journal de Voyages*, a magazine specializing in action-adventure fiction in a Vernian vein, and is to some extent adapted to that *milieu*, it is a cheerfully scathing political satire, a black comedy as funny as it is brutal. It might have compromised its own potential popularity by virtue of the generosity of its criticism—it spares no one the lash of its cynicism—but it is, by virtue of that fact, something of a minor masterpiece.

The second story that I have included here, as an eccentric companion-piece rather than a mere make-weight, was originally published in 1895 as *La deux fois morte*—which might also be translated as "The Woman Who Died Twice," although I have preferred a title that matches the deliberate terseness of the original, "Twice Dead." It was one of a number of novelettes that Lermina issued in pamphlet form through various publishers specializing in the occult. It too is a black comedy, which displays its cynicism in the voice of an unreliable narrator in much the same way as "Mystère-Ville," and with the same generosity of sarcasm. Like "Mystère-Ville," it offers a tantalizing glimpse of a kind of Utopia, which is callously destroyed by virtue of the willful blindness of those who cannot appreciate its value, although the incarnate dream is more fanciful and less pragmatic than the one hypothetically developed in the longer story, and might thus be reckoned less worthwhile.

This is the second volume of works by Jules Lermina that I have translated for Black Coat Press, following *Panic in Paris* (ISBN 978-1-934543-85-2; 2009),[1] and I included a detailed biography of the author in the earlier volume. There is no need to repeat all of its details here, but it is necessary for the reader to know the basic facts of the author's life in order to appreciate the two stories collected here as fully as they deserve.

Jules Hippolyte Lermina was born in 1839 and was still a child when the revolution of 1848 was followed by Louis-Napoléon's *coup d'état*, which launched in the Second Empire in 1851. He grew up as a dedicated opponent of that Empire, espousing a radical socialism that tended towards anarchism. Having married at eighteen, with a baby daughter to support, he tried his hand at various clerical jobs, but either could not settle into them or—perhaps more likely—could not hold on to them because of his political opinions, so he turned his hand to freelance journalism instead. His radicalism was as hazardous in that vocation as any other employment, by virtue of the relentless vigilance and oppressive policies of Napoléon III's censors, and he soon attracted their

---

[1] Black Coat Press also released Lermina's *To-Ho and the Gold Destroyers*, a 1905 proto-Tarzan novel, also published in *Le Journal des Voyages* (ISBN 978-1-935558-34-7).

attention. He founded a political periodical of his own, *Le Corsaire*, in 1867, which led to his being imprisoned. He was released in response to protest—from Victor Hugo, among others—but promptly repeated his crime, founding a new journal called *Satan*, and was imprisoned again.

By 1870, when the Second Empire collapsed following the disastrous French defeat by the Prussian army in the Battle of Sedan, Lermina knew his way around a courtroom and was thoroughly familiar with the temper of French justice. Although he was released from prison as soon as the new Government of National Defense took office, he immediately enlisted in the army, probably because that was the condition of his release. He was far from being a natural soldier—he was short, thin, pale, puny and of a somewhat nervous disposition even when not fresh out of prison—and his regiment, which engaged the enemy on at least two occasions, had no chance whatsoever of stemming the Prussian tide, although it did win one small victory, which is briefly commemorated in "Twice Dead."

Military discipline did not prevent Lermina from preparing campaign literature with which to stand for the proposed new National Assembly, before the promised elections were cancelled. He wrote an angry open letter of protest to the government when the chief protagonists of Communist agitation were imprisoned. Had he not been in the army, he would almost certainly have taken a hand in the subsequent insurrection, and might well have been transported along with its leaders when the Commune fell. As things were, the whole experience of the war and its aftermath seems to have been rather traumatic, and he took a new direction in life thereafter. He seems to have involved himself briefly in a project to form the communist colony of Aiglemont in the Ardennes, but his participation was brief; he was soon back in Paris, where he launched himself into a new career as a *feuilletonist*, producing popular fiction for various periodicals.

Although Lermina's political views did not change, he contented himself for the next two decades with simply making a living and supporting his family; his subsequent political journalism was more reflective in kind. He was still writing regularly for *Le Radical* in the 1890s, however, and his most significant work in that vein, the anarchist *L'ABC de Libertaire* [The ABC of Libertarianism] appeared not long after "Mystère-Ville," in 1906. His political beliefs are manifest in some of his other popular fiction, including *To-Ho le Tueur d'or* (1905; q.v.), but the bulk of his work consisted of rather slapdash crowd-pleasing entertainment, in the great tradition of the French *roman feuilleton*.

In his serial fiction Lermina set out conscientiously to serve as a loyal disciple of Eugène Sue and Alexandre Dumas; he wrote a Suesque *Mystères de New York* under the William Cobb pseudonym, and produced two sequels to *Le Comte de Monte Cristo*, as well as many other works in the same vein, almost all of which are nowadays long-forgotten. He did, however, obtain—and still retains—some reputation as a writer of graphic fantastic tales, of the sort collected in *Histoires incroyables* [Incredible Stories] (1885) and *Nouvelles histoires incroyables* [More Incredible Stories] (1888); that work drew praise from Isidore Ducasse, in his guise as the "Comte de Lautréamont," and (rather condescendingly) from Anatole France in one of the reviews collected in *La Vie littéraire*. Several of his stories in that vein were also signed "William Cobb," but in his later work he usually reserved it for stories set in America, or whose narrators posed as Americans; "Mystère-Ville" was an exception to this rule.

It is also useful for the reader to know certainly details of French history in order to appreciate "Mysteryville" fully. Although Lermina takes care to fill in the essentials within the text, he does skim lightly over certain matters with which readers outside France are less likely to be familiar, most importantly the Edict of Nantes and the career of Denis Papin.

The Edict of Nantes was issued in 1598 by Henri IV, who had escaped the St. Bartholomew's Day massacre of August 23, 1572—prompted by his marriage, while he was still Henri de Navarre, to Marguerite de Valois, the sister of the then king, Charles IX—by renouncing his Protestant faith and converting to Catholicism. Henri hoped that the edict, guaranteeing the Huguenots—French Protestants—the freedom to practice their religion without hindrance, would put an end to the persecution that had run rife in France since the Reformation began, and keep France out of the wars of religion that were running riot throughout Europe. In that respect, it was semi-successful, but the freedoms guaranteed by the edict were steadily eroded in the course of the next century, and it was eventually revoked entirely by Louis XIV in 1685, with the result that 400,000 Protestants (those who escaped the *dragonnades*—massacres carried out by Louis' cavalry) left France to go into exile.

Many of these exiles found refuge in Germany, although they were by no means made welcome there. They did, however, encounter other Huguenots who had left their homeland long before, in whose company they found some solace. These included Denis Papin, a scientist born in 1647 who had worked in Paris in the 1670s in collaboration with Christiaan Huygens and Gottfried Leibniz before going to England, where he worked with Robert Boyle on the compression of gases. As result of these researches he invented a steam "digester"—an early pressure-cooker equipped with a safety valve—and began to research further potential applications of steam power. He reported these results to the Royal Society in 1679, but went to Germany in 1687, where he built prototypes of a piston steam engine and a stream-powered boat, again working in collaboration with Leibniz. Alas, his efforts and plans came to nothing, for want of support.

During this period, Papin's correspondence with English scientists was read to the Royal Society without his permission and without due acknowledgement—probably because the then-president of the Society, Isaac Newton, loathed Leibniz and had a deep prejudice against anyone associated with him. While Papin was reduced to penury in the early years of the 18th century, Thomas Newcomen took advantage of his ideas to build the first practical steam engine, which was subsequently improved by James Watt, and whose exploitation eventually put England at the forefront of the Industrial Revolution.

How different the history of technology might have been if Papin had not been a despised exile, unwelcome in Germany and forbidden to return to his homeland, we can only guess—but what we know for certain is that he simply disappeared from human ken, all trace of him being lost. He is assumed to have died in 1712, alone and destitute, but there is no record of it. His uncertain fate provided Lermina with the perfect departure for the exercise in secret history mapped out in "Mystère-Ville," providing groundwork for the notion of an alternative technological development—a notion that is not taken entirely seriously in the story, but is taken just seriously enough to lend a hint of plausibility to the grotesque technological innovations on which its model anarchist utopia is founded.

It may also be useful, by way of introduction to "Mysteryville," briefly to note some of its literary antecedents. It was by no means the only story of its era to feature a hidden enclave in some remote corner of the Earth where exiles from an earlier civilization had constructed a technologically-advanced society. Although never as popular as fantasies of a converse sort, in which such fictitious enclaves retain survivals from various prehistoric eras, there are enough works of that sort to qualify as a subgenre.

The archetype of the subgenre—which Lermina had certainly read, because he makes explicit reference to it in the story I translated as "Panic in Paris"—was Edward Bulwer-Lytton's *The Coming Race* (1871, first issued anonymously), in which the inhabitants of the mysteriously-secluded enclave have attained a Utopia of sorts by virtue of their deployment of the force of *vril*, whose vagueness reflects the fact that it antedates the discovery of X-rays and radioactivity, when electrical technology as still in its infancy, and is deliberately confused with occult notions of "odic" force and "animal magnetism."

The Coming Race was a highly influential text, inspiring or influencing other exercises in kind, including several in the realm of popular fiction. The most notable is probably *Thoth* (1888), also published anonymously but actually the work of Joseph Shield Nicholson, which features an advanced civilization in the Egyptian desert founded by Homeric Greeks; Hume Nisbet's *Valdmer the Viking* (1893) only utilizes the motif in a subplot of relatively little interest. In a more serious and ambitious vein, *Limanora, the Island of Progress* (1903) by "Godfrey Sweven" (John Macmillan Brown)—a sequel to *Riallaro, the Archipelago of Exiles*, which features a whole series of utopian variants—is by far the most significant work in the subgenre, featuring the elaborate and conscientious development of a technological utopia.

Lermina is highly unlikely to have read any of the works written in English apart from *The Coming Race*, but their existence as kindred texts is nevertheless worth observing, if only as a testament to the extent to which the template provided by Bulwer remained in use between 1871 and 1903. Although I know of no close parallel texts in French prior to Lermina's, it is worth noting that there are certain similarities of theme and outlook between Lermina's text and a two-part story by Charles Nodier originally published in the *Revue de Paris* in 1833, which I translated as "Perfectibility" in the Black Coat Press anthology *The Germans on Venus*. Among other adventures, Nodier's hapless protagonist visits the island of the Patagons, where a dearth of resources has necessitated the development of chemical nutrition, as in Lermina's alternative Paris. In terms of the political views Nodier and Lermina were poles apart, but Lermina would certainly have appreciated Nodier's biting humor, and it seems quite probable that Lermina might have come across these two stories in a collection of Nodier's short fiction.

Whether Lermina read Nodier's couplet or not, he would certainly have been familiar with other futuristic Utopian satires in which refugees from modern Paris are enabled to visit advanced alternative versions of the city, including Louis-Sébastien Mercier's *Memoirs de l'an deux mille quatre cente quarante* (1771; rev. 1786; tr. as *Memoirs of the Year Two Thousand Five Hundred*) and—more pertinently—Emile Souvestre's scathingly sarcastic *Le monde tel qu'il sera* (1846; tr, as *The World As it Shall Be*). Albert Robida, who illustrated "Mystère-Ville" for the *Journal des Voyages*, had also produced some striking satirical visions of Paris in the mid-twentieth century, although he did not employ displaced narrators to view them with carefully-prejudiced nineteenth-century eyes. In displacing his own alternative Paris geographically, rather than temporally, Lermina was merely taking advantage of Bulwer's template to avoid the seeming necessity that condemned futuristic visions to the status of mere dreams, although he makes no attempt to avoid the quasi-hallucinatory aspects of his own vision, and is content to take some advantage of its ambiguity.

In political terms, Lermina is a long way to the left of Mercier, let alone Souvestre and Robida—although he shares Robida's pacifism—but it is worth noting that "Mystère-ville" appeared shortly before the most significant attempt by a French writer to produce an image of a communist utopia, which is contained in Anatole France's *Sur la pierre blanche* (1905; tr. as *The White Stone*). Since France was on record a decade before then giving grudging approval to Lermina's work, it is not impossible that he read "Mystère-Ville," and would surely have approved of it if he had, even though he preferred to do his own work in a much more earnest vein.

The biographical background to "Twice Dead" relates to an aspect of Lermina's life that was quite distinct from his political involvement, and arose almost by accident. Although his earliest works of fiction, written before he committed himself fully to professional writing, were heavily influenced by the works of Edgar Poe, as translated by Charles Baudelaire, Lermina had no interest in the supernatural at that time other than as a literary device, and he seems to have been a thoroughgoing materialist. Shortly after 1880, however, when she was in her early twenties, Lermina's daughter Marie-Pauline fell in love with and married one of the *bouquinistes* who ran bookstalls on the banks of the Seine, Henri Chacornac. Chacornac's stall specialized in occult literature.

Lermina presumably provided the financial backing for Chacornac to move up-market following the marriage; the couple opened a shop at 11 Quai Saint-Michel in 1884 under the title Librairie Générale des Science Occultes. The shop and its associated publishing enterprises were just in time to cash in on a remarkable explosion of interest in the occult, and they became very successful. Indeed, its descendent shops and publishing imprints remained the central pillar of that kind of French specialty publishing long into the twentieth century. The shop's *clientèle* included many literary men as well as would-be scholars and esoteric lifestyle fantasists, especially those associated with the nascent Decadent Movement, many of whom embraced occult themes enthusiastically. Lermina inevitably jumped on to the bandwagon, publishing *Le Comtesse Mercadet* (1884), the first of several stories about "animal magnetism," before assembling and filling out his two collections of *Histoires incroyables*.

Two of Chacornac's regular customers were medical students at the University of Paris who had been entranced by the works of the pioneering lifestyle fantasist

Eliphas Lévi (Alphonse-Louis Constant) and had been initiated into the esoteric discipline of "Martinism," founded by the 18th century mystic Martinez de Pasqually: Gérard Encausse and Augustin Chaboseau. Encausse, who used the signature "Papus" (borrowed from a document called the "Nuctemeron of Apollonius of Tyana," faked by Eliphas Lévi), went on to become one of the central figures of the Parisian occult revival, seemingly collecting Lermina along the way, just as he collected other potential publicists.

Encausse joined the French branch of the Theosophical Society shortly after its formation in 1884 but left within a year, dissatisfied with Madame Blavatsky's particular brand of mysticism. He then got together with two of Chacornac's other clients, Joséphin Péladan and Stanislaus de Guaita to form the Kabbalistique Ordre de la Rose-Croix. Their triple alliance did not last long, because Péladan split to form his own neo-Rosicrucian Order—which went on to enjoy tremendous success, completely eclipsing its forerunner—while Encausse, Guaita and Chaboseau revamped Martinism. Encausse took a leading role in a meeting held in April 1889 by 80 delegates of some 34 occult groups and societies to organize a massive "Spiritist Congress" that was held in Paris in September of that year; he persuaded Lermina to accept the honorary presidency of the congress and give the opening address.

Encausse went on to join the Parisian branch of the Order of the Golden Dawn and numerous other organizations, but was always outshone by Péladan, partly because the latter integrated a prolific and moderately successful career as a novelist into his career as a lifestyle fantasist. Eliphas Lévi had only turned to lifestyle fantasy when his own career as a *littérateur* had failed to take off, so it is hardly surprising that Encausse had literary ambitions too. He and Lucien Chamuel founded a publishing enterprise called the Librairie de Merveilleux in 1888, spearheaded by the periodical *L'Initiation*. There does not seem to have been any rivalry between Chacornac and Chamuel, even before Chacornac formally took over Chamuel's operation in 1901; the marketplace seems to have been large enough to accommodate them both comfortably. It was Chamuel who paid more attention to the literary aspects of the occult revival, publishing numerous works of fiction by Péladan, Jules Bois, Edouard Schuré and Jules Lermina (including *La Deux fois morte*); *L'Initiation* published fiction by such heroes of the Decadent Movement as Villiers de l'Isle-Adam and Catulle Mendès as well as work by Péladan, Bois and Lermina.

The literary spinoff of the occult revival, and the revisionist take on earlier supernatural fiction adopted by Encausse and other would-be critics, resulted in the perception that there was a new literary movement afoot, which Jules Huret—who conducted a long series of interviews for the *Echo de Paris* in 1891 in which he asked all the luminaries of French literature to speculate about its future direction—dubbed "Magism." He grouped his interviews with Péladan, Bois and Paul Adam together under the subheading "Les Mages." Anatole France also adopted the term, and identified Lermina as a "Magist" in discussing one of two Lermina novelettes to which "Papus" had provided a preface, *À brûler, conte astral* [For Burning; an Astral Tale] (1889)—the other was *L'Elixir de vie* (1890; tr. as "The Elixir of Life" in *Panic in Paris*). If Lermina was a "Magist" at all, however, he was certainly not the same kind of Magist as Péladan, whose fiction was in deadly earnest and flamboyantly propagandistic, or even Bois, who was a more sophisticated writer than Péladan and less credulous in his pose, but was nevertheless cut from the same cloth; Lermina was always careful to retain far more of what Poe called "the imp of the perverse" in his fiction. Although his signature appeared on a popular survey of *La Science occulte* (1890)—which might have had some input from Encausse—Lermina's involvement with the occult revival was always more social than philosophical, and occult romances were always a minor component of his output, which he never could take entirely seriously.

Encausse may have given up using Lermina as a collaborator simply because he no longer thought that "Papus" needed the publicity value of his name, but it is equally likely that he thought that his later exercises in neo-occult fantasy were too far off-message. *La Deux fois morte*, is a perfect example of Lermina's tendency to let his own skepticism show through too clearly, albeit rather slyly, to give his tales any persuasive force as popularizations of "occult science"—although it is certainly conscientious in putting the boot into skepticism itself, especially as represented by contemporary scientific orthodoxy.

The narrative template for *La Deux fois morte* was provided—as is acknowledged in the text—but "The Fall of the House of Usher," but it conscientiously updates the antiquarian materials of the earlier story, abandoning the Decadent preoccupation with degenerative heredity in favor of a motif borrowed from an obsessive theme contemporary "psychic research." It is notable, however, that Lermina does not refer his "spirit manifestation" back to Spiritualism, or use the term "ectoplasm," although he does use the term "séance" once, by way of slight acknowledgement. Indeed, Lermina provides an entirely original mock-theoretical basis for the speculative content of his story, making it close kin to his various exercises in scientific romance. What he does retain from Poe, however, is an intense interest in the psychological aspects of the manifestation, and the use of that psychological component to enhance the ambiguity of the story.

Because the female component of the triangular relationship featured in "Twice Dead" is a wife rather than a sister, eliminating suggestions of incest in favor of the kind of literary mythology of love promoted by such Romantic writers as Bernardin de Saint-Pierre, the sexual undercurrent of Lermina's story is quite distinct from that of Poe's, focused on the narrator's unadmitted but obviously powerful jealousy rather than the hero's guilt. That shift does, however, facilitate the development of the narrative's conscientious ambiguity, which is further enhanced by the deployment of ether—a substance whose hallucinatory potential had recently been abundantly celebrated in Jean Lorrain's cycle of the "*Contes d'un buveur d'éther*" (tr. in the Tartarus Press sampler *Nightmares of an Ether-Drinker*). Typically, Lermina does not use that ambiguity to refine the horror element of the story—and, indeed, he takes a brief moment to remind his readers that the original meaning of the term "horror" was not the meaning that it had acquired in the heyday of Gothic fiction—but to enhance the sarcasm of his tacit commentary on human self-deception and the irony of fate. Like "Mysteryville," "Twice Dead" is an essentially light-hearted work, which demands not to be taken too seriously, but its comedy is tinged with a deep shade of black, which serves to remind us, in no uncertain terms, that comedy is merely tragedy in a clown's mask.

The version of "Mystère-ville" that I used for translation was the Apex reprint; the version of *La Deux fois morte* was an electronic text available from ebooksgratuits.com. (A photographic reproduction of the first edition of the latter text is available on the Bibliothéque Nationale's gallica.com site, but is much harder to read than the elegantly-reset ebooksgratuits version.)

Brian Stableford

MYSTERYVILLE

I.

I have written these notes over a period of time. From the moment that I arrived in this singular land, I thought it appropriate to keep a daily journal.

Will this manuscript ever fall beneath the eyes of one of my former companions? I don't know. It is, in sum, for my personal use that I have written it, as if to convince myself of the reality of the extraordinary facts I have recorded.

I am familiar with human incredulity; if any European, any Parisian, were to read these lines, he would assess the observations and realities found herein as lies—and yet, there is not a single word that is not the expression of the pure truth.

Without further preamble, I shall get to the point.

I am a Frenchman, and a Parisian to boot. My parents, brave bourgeois who had scraped a meager living in a modest clothing shop, left me an orphan as I approached my twentieth year. I had obtained a rather rudimentary education, without taking much account of the advice given to me by my mother, being overfond of the instruction of others.

Something that might appear strange at first, but is, in truth, more common than is generally believed, is that my father, sedentary by vocation, calm by disposition and mollycoddled by my mother—who had not allowed him to venture beyond the suburbs of Paris for fear of accidents—dreamed constantly of voyages, distant expeditions and the exploration of mysterious lands. His only vice—sternly opposed by my ever-anxious mother—consisted of buying maps, books and periodicals related to voyages. Livingstone had filled him with enthusiasm; he had dreamed about Binger; he shivered at the name of Nordenskjöld; and became feverish at the thought of Nansen.[2]

He had rented an attic on the sixth floor of the house under the pretext of storing cloth and so-called novelty fabrics for making suits, overcoats or waistcoats, but the choice of an elevated floor was Machiavellian, my mother's obesity militating against the ascent. In reality, it was a library, a lumber-room of all imaginable collections and tales, authentic or legendary. It was so cluttered that, in order to keep one's balance, it was necessary to set one foot on the North Pole and the other on the Cape of Good Hope, while supporting oneself with one hand in Manchuria and the other in the United States National Park. One trampled the world underfoot there, and sat down on the universe.

Now, my brave father had very easily made me into his disciple. I spent long hours huddled in that redoubt, which seemed to be a synthesis of the Earth. With my knees bent and my back aching, I would plunge myself

---

[2] David Livingstone (1813-1873) explored the territories to either side of the Zambezi river. Louis-Gustave Binger (1856-1936) explored the Niger River and the Ivory Coast. Nils Nordenskjöld (1832-1901) discovered the North-East Passage from the North Sea to the Pacific. Fritjof Nansen (1861-1930) explored Greenland and the Arctic Sea.

into that multitudinous crowd of old books, which might have qualified as a vagabond's manuals.

The most bizarre thing is that I was utterly ignorant of geography. I could have recited chapter and verse concerning the mores of the Kirghiz or the customs of the Somalis, but it would have been impossible for me to say exactly where their native lands were. For me, the Earth was a huge sack into which peoples and regions were thrown pell-mell, into which one slid one's hand as into a bran tub, at random, with the certainty of drawing out some marvel. Naturally, I ended up conceiving a maritime vocation. I even had the audacity, beneath my father's tender eye, of talking in front of my mother about a possible engagement on a ship of state. Oh yes, that went down well!

My poor, dear parents. They disappeared within two months of one another, leaving me and the business fairly well stocked, and nice lot of gilt-edged orders to fill. Needless to say, I did not hesitate for a moment to liquidate the lot and transform it into hard currency, ready to roll—as I was myself—around the world.

For five years I made it my business—which no one else would have accepted, even if they had paid dearly for it, but which delighted me—to be incessantly on the move, without stopping, from one city to another, by means of railways and ferry-boats, trams and motor cars. I did not make a tour of the world; that phrase evokes the idea of a circle, which bears no resemblance to my method of procedure, whose whimsicality was indescribable. I was an unrepentant zigzagger, going from North to South and West to East according to my caprice and my curiosity, always in search of a new emotion, following a broken line, without any plan, with unexpected reversals of direction, illogical flights and unmotivated pauses.

Now, do you know what exceedingly strange impression these journeys, continually changing direction, made on me? In truth, nothing astonished me. Never, no matter what country I was in, did I have any sensation of novelty, of the unknown. Engravings and photographs had already revealed the interesting sights to me, and no matter what monument or panorama confronted me, a disenchanted "I knew that!" rose to my lips. I counted myself fortunate when I was unable to tell myself silently, as I did before the pyramids of Egypt, that they looked much better in photographs.

Fundamentally, everything resembles everything else. Anyone who has seen Paris, Venice, Constantinople and any agglomeration of Arab tents has seen it all. He will rediscover the same impressions everywhere; whether a bay is that of Naples, Lisbon or Buenos Aires, the emotion one feels is always identical. Questions of degree are insignificant. The Sun is not without monotony, whether it burns furiously, as in the tropics, or pales, as in the Scandinavian countries.

Most of all, consideration always struck me that, in sum, for anyone capable of reasoning, the progress of affairs obeys rules that are the same everywhere and always produces, with greater or lesser advancement, analogous results. Thus is it with nocturnal lightning: resin torches, wax candles, oil-lamps, kerosene, gas and electricity form phases of a progress whose stages one finds everywhere. Tell me how you light your home and I will tell you the phase of civilization at which you have arrived.

I will add that the development of illustration has been fatal to the sensation of curiosity; the ancient explorers happening upon Toltec ruins, the alignments of Karnak, Muslim minarets or Buddhist pagodas experienced a genuine shock. The last man to have felt it was probably the happy mortal for whom an excursion through the Cambodian jungle put him in the presence of the monuments of Angkor Wat. Today, however, there is no ten-year-old infant who is not familiar with these perspectives and silhouettes. So what? It is the story of the peasant who comes to Paris and recognizes the palaces of which we are so proud as the subjects of postcards hawked by traveling salesmen.

In brief, I can affirm that not once, during my five years of hectic excursions, was I able to escape the impression of having seen it all before.

I continued my search, however, incessantly—and in May 1900 I fetched up in China, at Peking, where I found yet again the inevitable pagoda, the perpetual coolie, the legendary palanquin, along with—O horror!—railways, the telegraph and the banal industries of iron, smelting and steel. I already knew that domestic servants wear hats, that the Chinese take off their spectacles in order to talk to someone, that the best brought-up people spit on the carpet, that one of their greatest politenesses is to take salt between the index-finger and the thumb and sprinkle it over your food, that they throw the bones under the table, and that they terminate a meal with gestures of relief that are as singular as they are noisy. All that did not constitute, so far as I was concerned, one of those surprises that compensate for any and all fatigue.

So, having dragged my boots from the Gate of Peace, Ngang-Tin-Men, to Tien-Men, the Gate of the Dawn and from the Gate of Submission, Pin-Tse-Men, to Tong-Che-Men, the Gate of the East, having wandered from the Pagoda of the Learned to the Mountain of

27

Coal—Mec-Chaen—I felt myself gripped, for the first time, by a profound discouragement.

I was frightfully bored, and nothing was able to dissipate the moral dullness that oppresses and depresses one. In vain, I stood for hours on the Marble Bridge, watching the noisy and heterogeneous crowd pass by; in vain, I tried to interest myself in the Blue Pagoda with the thousand little bells that chime in the wind, in Nam-Tang and its cathedral, the towers of which resemble the arms of a giant reaching for the sky. The bizarre monuments, the exotic mores, the civilization so different from ours, and yet fundamentally so analogous, left me with no other sensation than intellectual weariness.

Where should I go now? To Siberia? I would find the footprints of Westerners beneath its snows. To Japan? It was becoming civilized! To Cambodia or Annam? I would rub shoulders there with functionaries and watch the unpacking of merchandise fabricated in the Faubourg Saint-Denis or Birmingham, if not Berlin or Stuttgart!

Was it true, then, as the ancients used to say, that there was nothing new under the sun, and that the planet could no longer offer me a spectacle that I would enjoy or even—for I would have much preferred it to monotony—to terrify me?

Suddenly, a thought occurred to me.

Why was I astonished to find great centers of population identical to one another, save for minor differences of customs and mores? A Chinese, albeit in spite of his atavistic resistance, is no less submissive than any other man to the irresistible penetration that operates between different beings; as in plants, there is a sort of osmosis that occurs, of which those whom it modifies are unaware. I told myself, however, that the Chinese

28

peasant—an agriculturalist, or even a savage; in brief, the natural Chinese—would be interesting to study; that perhaps, in the midst of those primitives not yet submissive to rules that go back 50 centuries, I might find myself in confrontation with some unexpected mental manifestation, or, at the very least, a sight as yet unclassified and uncatalogued in books.

I ought to add that, during my indefatigable peregrinations, I had at least acquired a precious faculty, somewhat akin to the gift of tongues; after a few months, in whatever country I found myself, I could understand and express myself with a facility at which I marveled. It was like an almost-immediate intuition, as if there existed within me a memory of having spoken the language before, in a previous life, which was now reborn by some means in my brain cells.

To cut a long story short, I left Peking and resolved to launch myself westwards into the unknown reaches of China, as far away as possible from the sea and European communications. My plan was very simple; I would simply go forth, in a half-Chinese half-Manchu costume that would not attract attention—which would not be difficult, so indifferent are the Chinese to everything—and install myself somewhere on the western frontier, beyond the Great Wall, in the region of Dun-Khou, on the river Houang-Ho. I had hired a few servants, on whom I thought I could reply absolutely, and I had an abundant supply of money. I had, moreover, decided to live alone. I had not yet experienced isolation. Who could tell whether it might not have surprises in store for me?

It did, indeed, have some surprises in store for me, as will be seen as the story progresses…

I was lucky, in one respect.

Dun-Khou, which I reached after two days ride, is a large village, quite respectable, as it happens—and which, unfortunately for itself, is well-known even to those who have never heard its name; it is the village depicted on screens, whose houses have pointed roofs ornamented with bells, built of red wood, with its beautiful blue lake and its large birds, which seem painted for the pleasure of the eyes by an ornamentalist.

I took up residence at the utmost extremity of the town, beyond a little bridge—which you can see by closing your eyes—and there, in the midst of my books, I set to work assiduously reading the works of Khong-Fong-Tseu, whom we have baptized Confucius for our own convenience.

Oddly enough, I felt the ambitions of a Sinologist awakening within me. I even mapped out an interesting program of study. I wanted, by going back through the scientific history of China, to study the condition of its ancient civilization, to take exact account of the progress that it had once realized, when, we are told, it had invented—well before Europeans—printing, the compass and gunpowder. I wanted to know the truth about those legends, and, finally, to discover the true causes of the sudden interruption of that civilization; to find the pebble that had stopped the machine...

At Dun-Khou, there was an old mandarin who was by no means an imbecile, and who, in spite of my European condition, did not hesitate to form a relationship with me. Curious, erudite and rather broad-minded, Fo-Hi-Li, as he was called, became inseparable from me, almost my friend, and had I not sometimes caught a glimpse—doubtless mistaken—of a singular expression of malicious irony in his slanting eyes, I would have blessed the hazard that had caused me to encounter a man worthy of all sympathy, after such a long search. I shall, however, press on to the catastrophe to which everything precedent is no more than a preamble.

I worked; I went walking with Fo-Hi-Li; I tried to chat about this and that to the laborers; I caressed the little children and demonstrated a particular predilection for the pink pigs, reminiscent of playthings, that constituted the wealth of the region. I will not say that people threw their arms around me or heaped smiles upon me; the Chinese are cold, and, for a European, it is sufficient not to be in disgrace to appreciate the forbearance of the indigenes. Besides, Fo-Hi-Li was my patron and protector, and, after having been wandering for such a long time, I went to sleep peacefully in that bed of placidity, so softly that I almost got to the point of dreaming of an entire life unfolding nonchalantly on the banks of the Huang-Ho.

One night, though—it was in the second week of June 1900[3]—I was woken with a start by a strange sensation. I had been dreaming that savages had taken me prisoner and were roasting me in front of a hot fire—but it seemed to me that my dream corresponded closely with reality when, on opening my eyes, I saw that I was surrounded by a red light of the most deplorable appearance.

Fire! My house was burning! Within an instant— one's faculties are multiplied tenfold at such moments— I perceived that the flames were surrounding me on all sides, as if the fire had been lit simultaneously in every

---

[3] The so-called "Boxer rebellion" against European colonialists in China began on June 13 1900 and continued until August 14, when an international army relieved the legations in Peking.

corner of the house. The building was made of wood—which is to say that it offered no resistance, and that, within a few minutes, I could and probably would be charred like a chicken that had fallen into a blacksmith's forge.

There is no point in detailing my actions; they can easily be guessed. I seized my clothes and dressed in all haste. Then I leapt to my feet, shouted for help and threw myself at hazard, blindly, toward the first exit that presented itself: a door or a window—I have no idea. What I shall never forget, though, was the shrill, strident, horrible clamor that went up when my silhouette stood up amid the flames. Was it pity, encouragement or hope? If the slightest doubt persisted within me, it quickly vanished, for the crowd was composed of all the people of the village, at whose head a distinctly recognized my excellent friend Fo-Hi-Li, who was yelling, even louder than the rest: "Death to the Frenchman! Death to the foreign devil!"

I ought to say that for some time, rumors of revolt and massacres of Europeans, had been reaching my ears. There was talk of secret societies—the Boxers—bent on exterminating all white men, but my perfect mandarin Fo-Hi-Li had laughed with me at that crazy and ridiculous prospect. Now the traitor had cast his mask aside; I was, and had always been, the enemy. I had been shown the truth.

The situation was doubly critical; if I persisted in staying inside my house, I would be rapidly reduced to the state of a cinder; if I went out, I would fall beneath the pikes, staffs and claws of those yellow rogues. The tongues of flame were darting toward me; a few more seconds and I would be trapped by the fire. It was, therefore, necessary for me not to indulge in a long meditation and to weigh coolly—coolly, above all!—the pros and cons.

I decided abruptly to attempt the impossible. After all, being certain of dying if I took no action, there remained one chance—in a thousand—of saving myself by acting. So, leaping through the midst of the flames, I raced through the crowd of Chinamen. Don't ask me what I did or how I did it. The truth is that, without knowing anything, and without understanding anything, my memory retaining nothing but the terrible vision of an astonishing mêlée of brandished weapons, writhing arms, tangles and contortions, the whole thing being nothing more than nightmare and madness…until I found myself one morning—or one evening, I'm damned if I know!—lying face down, with my arms and legs describing a Saint Andrew's Cross, and my nose in the dirt.

That much I know, for I had at first the ineffable joy of a resurrection—but as I tried to compose my thoughts, to attempt to understand where I was and where I was going, darkness fell once again upon my brain. Fear—a terrible fear—shook me, galvanized me and launched me forwards, without the intervention of my will or my initiative…and I had a sensation of running, running for hours on end, perhaps for entire days, without it being possible for me to recall anything but the monotonous and brutal rhythm of two feet striking the ground more rapidly, ever more rapidly…

I do not believe that I stopped for a single instant, but I could not swear to it. Certainly, I had neither drank nor eaten anything. I was like an automaton with a broken spring, whose mechanism was running on and on. I ran; I trotted; I galloped furiously, like a madman who has escaped from his padded cell…until the moment when I felt a blow on my head, as if I had been hit on top of my skull by a staff…

The mechanism faltered, jammed and snapped, and I fell to the ground, inert and inanimate: broken…dead.

II.

Was I dead?

No, for dead men feel no pain, and I was conscious of my existence by virtue of the stabbing pains that were shooting through all my limbs. Yes, yes, I was alive, having the conviction that my arms and legs were broken, and that my shoulders were dislocated. And my head! It was aching so much that I hesitated to move it, so fearful was I that the pieces of my skull might come apart, each falling in a different direction...

More hours passed before I recovered possession of my faculties. From time to time, there was a sort of lurch inside my skull, as if a surge were bringing me back to life, followed by prostration and numbness...

To tell the truth, I was hovering between the alternatives of life and death; perhaps a sick man, in his death throes, experiences such bizarre intervals...

How long did that anguish last? It is impossible for me to measure it, however approximately. Finally, it calmed down conclusively; I recovered my self-possession, my reason, my intellect. I understood that I could think normally, and only then did I obtain quite clearly and profoundly, the idea of a resurrection.

At first, I did not think to ask where I was; my initial curiosity, quite naturally, was to check what state my poor carcass was in. I attempted to move my limbs, one by one; one leg proved immediately capable of flexion. I scarcely dared try the other, telling myself that one of the two must surely be broken, but I took the chance. The second, like the first, was intact. So was the right arm! And the left!

That exploration of my own body was most interesting. I raised my hands to my head, expecting the bony container of my cranium to give way beneath my fingers. Not at all! It was solid. My nose, too! And my eyes! Everything seemed to be intact, and in place.

Suddenly, I shivered. I was lying on my back, on a hard material that had to be rock. I told myself that it was my back that was broken, and that I would be incapable of standing up...

That thought was so painful that I was convinced, at first, that I had made the necessary verification that that my paralysis was henceforth entirely certain...and I had a strong desire to weep. But no! But no! I had not made the inquisitive effort! Oh, with what tightness in my chest I placed my two hands flat on the ground, to provide a point of support for my elevation. I uttered a cry of joy. I was sitting up! Yes, sitting up! Then, abruptly, I arched my back—which did not give way—and I stood up.

To understand the astonishing joy that ran through my veins and arteries like a warm stream, you would have had to have undergone something similar. In fact, I would not wish it on my worst enemy. It is true that the compensation was enormous; to feel oneself alive, not crippled or lame, when one has been the plaything of chance and madness for a time one cannot measure, a dead leaf borne away by a hurricane, which might have been reduced to dust...

I was, therefore, standing up—very weary, to be sure, my muscles slack, my head half-empty, but, all things considered, already certain that rest was all that was needed to repair the damage...

Rest—and nourishment! For my first sensation was that of an intense hunger.

Imagine that, when I tried to calculate the time that had elapsed since my flight from Dun-Khou, I could not, with all possible moderation and appealing to all my self-composure, estimate it at less than three or four days—which is to say that, in the state of insouciance into which surprise, terror and the instinct of self-preservation had cast me, I had probably accomplished the feat of running for 24 or 48 hours, which might represent 50 or 60 leagues! It seems impossible, and yet…

It is understandable that, for the moment, in that first phase of awakening, I did not devote myself to such calculations. Only the distress of my stomach, the sharp pangs of hunger, provided evidence of the extent of the crisis. For the first quarter of an hour, I remained still, my mind focused on that single problem: eating! It obsessed me to the extent that I could not think about anything else—not even finding a means to discover some nourishment. Such mental disturbances are incredible. The shocks I had undergone and the suffering I was presently experiencing produced a sort of hypnotism or catalepsy in me.

Finally, my brain woke up again, and there was a glimmer of light in my head. I opened my eyes—or, rather, checked that they were open and clarified them, because they had been open all the while but had been neither gazing nor seeing—and I uttered a cry of astonishment, almost of horror.

The place where I was could only be described by one phrase: a passage at the bottom of an abyss.

I understood immediately why my visual sense had been so slow to recover its acuity. In the narrow space in which I was enclosed, between two granite walls that rose up to a prodigious height, there was nothing but a grey, diffuse light, scarcely sufficient for it to be possible to discern objects. When I raised my head, in the instinctive movement of animals and flowers searching for light, I saw—above me, but at such a height that I could not even attempt to estimate it—a strip of bright blue sky, illuminated by a sun so ardent that it was almost white.

I raised my arms toward that light, toward the sun that I could not see. It was like a promise of life, a hope of salvation—but that was an illusion; the terrible reality gripped me again. How had I got into that rocky fissure, that crevasse less than three meters wide?

My emotion was such that I no longer felt hunger. All my vitality was concentrated in the notion of danger, the desire to escape.

To begin with, what could these rocks be? I knew that for twenty leagues around—and in all of western China, for that matter—the country was absolutely flat. The province of Ordos, which it is necessary to cross to get from Peking to Dun-Khou, is nothing but a vast plain, and beyond the Houang-Ho River, Mongolia begins. Then there is the Gobi desert, with its extents of sand, where caravans scarcely dare to go—the desert which, it is said, was born from a cataclysm analogous to the sinking of Atlantis, whose approaches are defended not only by the sinister harshness of the wilderness but also by legends that the Chinese and Mongols will only relate in lowered voices.

I tried to summon up my geographical memories, but the cerebral effort only served to increase my perplexity. It was impossible that I had come back in the direction of the Great Wall, toward Yu-Lo, for in traversing the Chinese countryside I would inevitably have perished in the hands of fanatics. On the other hand, though, if I had taken the direction of the Gobi…I could not have reached any mountains that way.

But what was the point of reasoning? Either it was necessary to resign myself to a slow death by hunger, or I had to gather all my energy into a decisive effort, to act and struggle…

Suddenly, my resolution was so firm and vigorous that I no longer felt my hunger or my fatigue. I wanted to live, and that determination pulled me together, affirmed by a nervous vigor that took on the appearance of an actual force.

I examined the corridor in which I was imprisoned by two lateral walls. To think of climbing them would have been the height of folly; they were sheer, and made of a material that seemed to me to be volcanic, a black basalt with a smooth surface. There remained the two directions of the corridor. By reason of the dearth of light, it was impossible for me to distinguish anything more than a few meters away; it was therefore necessary for me to undertake an exploration, commenced at hazard.

Having taken a few steps, however, I perceived that the ground, formed by a black mass identical to the walls, was sloping; instinctively, doubtless because I hoped to escape from the abyss by going upwards, I started walking up the slope. I did so, in my estimation, for about a kilometer.

At first the slope was almost imperceptible, perhaps two or three centimeters per meter. Mechanically comparing the ascensional progress thus obtained to the height of the rocks, which I estimated to be at least 150 or 160 meters, I was beginning to tell myself that I would never arrive at a summit when a something happened that would have dispelled any illusion, had any remained to me.

The two walls suddenly drew closer, to the point of scarcely leaving me the room necessary to pass through facing forwards. I set myself sideways and hazarded a few more steps. I experienced a sensation of choking, of crushing; I even had the horrible thought that if I went any further forward it might be impossible for me to get back again. I would be gripped, held fast by the rocks and would die there—an exceedingly slow and horrible death.

My blood froze, but the weakness was fleeting. I succeeded in recovering my composure and, turning round, started walking again, down the slope. In fact, that was much more logical. If I were to find help at all, it would doubtless be more probable that I would find it on the plain than those inaccessible peaks, where no human being was likely ever to have set foot.

Thus, it was with an open mind and without any despair that I retraced my steps—except that I hurried even faster, for it seemed to me that the strip of sky that was above my head was becoming less luminous. Perhaps night was falling—and if so, what would become of me in the darkness? I did not even want to think about that.

I was almost running now, being in haste to escape the embrace of those vertical walls, of which I was afraid, as if—I remembered Edgar Poe's "The Pit and the Pendulum"—they might suddenly come together to crush me.

In the semi-obscurity that surrounded me, optical illusions sometimes showed me a sudden parting of the rocks, or even a distant glimmer of light at the far end of the corridor. A few more paces and there would be liberty, life…

No; the route went on interminably, sometimes sloping upwards, sometimes descending again, almost sheer, until the moment—oh, how did I not die of rage and despair?—when I bumped into an enormous boulder, a fragment of the mountain that had crumbled away…and which blocked the way completely.

Yes, I was trapped! No exit! I fell upon that stone cube, which must have weighed several thousand kilos, and tried with my hands and fingernails to tear it out of the black recess that retained it.

Nothing! The most powerful machines could not have budged it.

Oh, then the fever of terror that had already possessed me seized me once again. I rushed at the rock as if it were possible to climb over it, or as if my limbs might suddenly be furnished with adhesive suction-cups capable of attaching them to the smooth basalt. Twenty times I fell back; 20 times more I launched myself forward.

Then seized by despair, maddened, understanding that it was all over, I started running again, using my hands to feel the wall whose two sides imprisoned me…going at top speed only to slow down a moment later, to proceed one step at a time, my neck extended, my eyes questing.

Night fell—the definitive darkness that would be, for me, that of the tomb.

Exhausted, impotent, I stood still, as if stunned, with an incessant thundering in my brain. And hunger—the hunger that gripped my entrails once again…

I seemed to be sinking into the shadow and the silence.

Throughout my being, I experienced such agony—compounded out of despair and the exasperated tension of my muscles—that, no longer being in control of myself, I began howling with all my might, stupidly shouting for help, begging some invisible and all-powerful being to come to my aid.

Suddenly, I heard a singular noise, like something sliding along the basalt wall; there was an echo of friction, of a soft murmur. I felt my hair stand up on my head. I had my back to the wall, looking hard with wide-open eyes into that shadow, where I now dreaded to see…what?

This: some sort of enormous reptile, stouter than my own body, whose skin was brightened by a phosphorescence—and which was descending, doubtless suspended by its tail from some crack in the rock.

That semi-luminous thing, which seemed as if it were endowed with some intimate faculty of radiation, was swaying. I could see its head, or what I believed to be its head. It had no eyes, but a mouth like the orifice of a fire-hose, something like the maw of an octopus, which was moving back and forth, as if in search of prey…

Ten times that horrible and fantastic monstrosity passed in front of me, almost over me. I flattened myself against the stone, enraged that it did not open up to allow me passage…and the mouth finally settled upon me.

I had an overwhelming impression of invincible suction and, as if breathed in by the monster, I was lifted into the air.

In that astonishing moment, days and weeks ran by…and in my recovered placidity, in the perfect happiness that I now enjoy, I can no longer evoke the memory of that ascension without experiencing a sharp, general ill-feeling similar to that which accompanies nightmare episodes.

The mighty serpent—for how can I give any other name to that long rounded body?—hoisted me steadily upwards along the wall, which my limbs scarcely brushed.

I did not experience any pain, but my anguish was atrocious.

The beast had seized me by the shoulders, at the base of the neck, and I went up in a vertical stance, rather like a cat whose neck has been gripped by a strong hand—but I neither resisted nor thought of struggling; like an animal loaded on to a ship with the aid of straps passed under its belly, I let myself hang limply, arms and legs inert.

Suddenly there was something like a swirling wind around me, and it was horrible painful. From the still atmosphere in which I had remained for so long at the bottom of the crevasse I felt myself transported into an active environment, a moving atmosphere. It seemed to me that I had been turned around, since I had begun to descend again. I was not falling; I was still firmly held by the round mouth what was hermetically fixed to my flesh. I was at the end of my tether, though; my intellect could no longer hold out....

The last impression that I had was this: having touched the ground, or believing that I had, I saw in front of me, beneath a bizarre light whose nature was incomprehensible to me, a house, with a sign on which I read the words: *Hôpital Saint-Martin*.[4]

Evidently, I had gone mad. I fainted.

---

[4] The Hôpital Saint-Martin is a military hospital in Paris, situated just across the road from the Gare de l'Est.

III.

Of the period following that event, it is hardly surprising that no precise memory remains to me. My entire being had been turned upside-down by a shock so violent that my fibers, muscles, nerves, the lobes of my brain and the most infinitesimal particles of my organism were in as state of complete disequilibrium.

It seemed to me that a process of disaggregation was taking place within me, as if all the cells making up my body had been mobilized and were running into one another, mingling and colliding. If water being drunk could experience a sensation, that is what it would be like.

At the same time, rapid visions succeeded one another with vertiginous promptitude, streaming before my internal eyes. It was like an exhibition of cinematography, showing me, alongside real individuals and objects, creations of dream and nightmare.

In simpler terms, I shall say that I was prey to the delirium of a fever—and that delirium was so intense that its suggestions took on all the characteristics of reality; I saw once again, in an astonishing composite synthesis, all the regions through which I had traveled. The scenes were juxtaposed and blended together. The churches of Moscow rose up in the Place de la Concorde; I found Notre-Dame on the shore of a Scandinavian fjord, the Acropolis in the gardens of Cintra, near Lisbon, New York's Broadway extending as far as the eye could see into the Sahara and the bayaderes of Jagganath dancing on an iceberg in the Behring Sea, while the gauchos of La Plata served soup at London's Criterium: a stupefying confusion and an activity so formidable that it imposed a painful strain on my attentive faculties.

At one particular moment, the saraband of illusion became so frenzied that my head almost burst: the geographical scenes had been succeeded by industrial scenes, and there was nothing in my brain but whirling machines, levers like the arms of knights errant, crankshafts in perpetual motion, pistons growing to giant size in order to crush one another like dwarfs...

Gas blazed, kerosene fumed, electricity crackled. My nerves were stretched like wires through which indefatigable vibrations coursed at high pressure: a veritable torture, compared with which the most ingenious tortures of the most subtle executioners would have been pleasures.

Suddenly, it seemed to me that there was a gentle breath passing through my entire body, like a spring breeze—and, curiously enough, it was not an external impression that I was experiencing, but a penetrating, intimate sensation, which bore no resemblance to any sensation with which I was familiar...

How can I define it? It was simultaneously luminous and musical, like a filtrate of color and sound that entered into me through every pore, insinuating itself into the most secret recesses of my organs. Yes, one might have thought it a vaporization of melodic, colored, even perfumed atoms, which infiltrated me, along with an exquisite sedation.

My physical exaltation gradually thinned out; the whirlwind of my sensations showed down; the stabbing pains that had been shooting through me a little while before were transformed into caresses—and I opened my eyes, at the same time as I recovered the power of thought.

Around me there was a physical atmosphere, a very faint mauve in color, with a background of tints fading into one another as in a rainbow, ranging from celestial blue to a pure and serene violet. At the same time, a sound struck my ears, which was neither that of familiar instruments—harps, violins or oboes—nor that of human voices, but which nevertheless partook of all those harmonies: something inexpressibly sweet.

There was one more thing, quite exquisite and very difficult to express: a flotation of perfume, which surrounded me like an imponderable aromatic down, a fluid of volatilized scent, in which I found the most tenuous and scarcely discernible essences of roses, lilies and balsamic resin—or, rather, of everything that was not that, but a vapor made of all vapors, distilled and sublimated to the point of being nothing more than an odorant ambience.

I felt myself cradled by that triple sensation of color, music and perfume—and it was a delightful pacification. I noticed that these actions were not being exercised upon me in a monotonous and essentially indifferent fashion. Sometimes the melody was accentuated, becoming more rhythmic, rendering a tonicity to my muscles that effort tended to affirm; sometimes the color, more vivid, gripped my eyes, arousing my faculty of vision more intensely, then softened again, as its shades faded, returning to its natural level.

I had always been something of a Sybarite; I confess without shame that I have never been penetrated more delightfully by the subtlety of physical enjoyment and, at the same time, mental languor. I was not doing anything, or thinking anything; I was savoring my resurrection, as I had often lingered voluntarily in the numb semi-sleep that precedes a definitive awakening.

Suddenly, however, I perceived that the rhythm of the music, still discreet, as if coming through a wall of cotton wool, became more active. A red dot was added to the delicate tints of my atmosphere, and, at the same time, I perceived quite distinctly the perfume of vervain.

Then I raised myself up on my elbow and looked around.

I was in a high-ceilinged room whose walls were made of a transparent substance that was not glass, but which I could not yet identify. Colonnettes of stucco, marble and other unidentifiable materials framed and retained the panels—and it was through those singular windows that an iridescent light was filtering. Cassolettes made of porphyry and onyx, or analogous minerals, were discharging perfumes, while an invisible orchestra melodized the atmosphere.

"Where am I?" I cried.

Then, at the foot of the item of furniture on which I was lying, I saw a very singular individual—to sum him up in a single phrase, a Molièresque physician, with a long robe and pointed hat. He leaned toward me, and said:

"How are you feeling, milord stranger?"

IV.

If this manuscript—anything is possible—should ever arrive in the hands of a Frenchman, he is bound to have been present at a performance of *Le Médecin malgré lui*, or some other masterpiece by our great comic author; thus, he will have had before his eyes the legendary character of the physician that I saw at my bedside in flesh and bone. He was not ridiculous, though; his face was rather handsome and very serious, and his expression was benevolent.

I greeted him, and replied: "*Monsieur le docteur*, I know that I must have been very ill, but it seems to me that, at present, my condition is greatly ameliorated."

"I'm very glad to hear it," the unknown replied.

I beg the reader to remember, briefly, what has gone before. I was in China. The Boxers had burned my house and tried to murder me. Seized by a convulsive fear that soon degenerated into a nervous crisis, I had launched into a mad, delirious flight whose duration and vicissitudes I could not remember. I had fallen down, worn out, exhausted and dying. I had found myself interred in a black gorge, in which I could do no more than await death, my ineffectual efforts only succeeding in making my despair more atrocious. When I finally saw a hideous monster appear, whose implausible ugliness multiplied the horror of an imminent ingurgitation a hundredfold, I was seized and lifted up. I had not even had the last resort of defending myself, unable to make the heroic sacrifice of a life that no longer belonged to me. I had heard nothing for months but the Chinese language; I knew that for hundreds of leagues around me there was no one but Orientals, Hindus, Englishmen and Russians…and here I am, face to face with a doctor who reminds me, in his gravity, of Coquelin Cadet,[5] and is questioning me in excellent French as to the state of my health. Admit that the incident is far from banal, and that I was bound to wonder whether I was not mad, and whether all of it was not a figment of my deranged imagination.

I lay there, astounded, my eyes wide open, looking at that costume—which, although fashioned in a manner that was not unfamiliar to me, seemed to be made of a strange fabric, as black and shiny as anguish and just as stiff, while the tall hat seemed to be made of a furry metal, substituting for felt.

"Monsieur," I said, abruptly, "would you care to tell me, first of all, whether I am dead or alive?"

The individual smiled very kindly. He gestured with his hand, doubtless bidding me to be patient. Then he went to the back of the room, opened a little cupboard, and took out an instrument that resembled and might have been mistaken for a coquette's atomizer. He put it in my hand and said: "Apply your olfactory organ to that little orifice." At the same time, he lifted my hand up to the level of my face and stuck the end of a short tube up my nostril.

Instinctively, and having no reason to refuse, I sniffed—and a gaseous jet rose up, beyond the root of my nose, penetrating as far as the meninges.

Having taken out the tube, I said: "Excuse me, Monsieur. I know that I'm alive."

---

[5] The actor Ernest Coquelin (1848-1909), a star of the Parisian stage, was known as Coquelin Cadet to distinguish him from his elder brother Constant.

His gesture expressed satisfaction. "In that case, Monsieur le Comte," he said in his turn, "you're able to listen to me and explain yourself..."

"Explain myself!" I cried. "But isn't it me who's entitled to explanations? Once again, where am I? And why are you addressing me as Monsieur le Comte?" I had always been democratically minded, and that appellation wounded me.

He adopted an astonished expression. "Are you not a gentleman?" he asked me.

"I don't even know what you mean by the word, which is no longer current in the language I speak."

"But which is surely the French language?"

"Obviously," I said, slightly irritated.

"Now, in our time," he went on, "a man of your appearance and your education had to be a gentleman."

"In your time!" I retorted, more and more astonished. "I'm damned if I know what you mean. In my time—which is to say, today—those vain denominations...gentleman, Comte, even Duc...no longer have any rational or precise significance."

He remained silent for a while, profoundly reflective. Then he said: "Forgive me my indiscretion, and please don't be offended by my words...but I'd like to know..."

"What?"

"Which descendant of Louis XIV is reigning over France today?"

"Descendant of...!" In truth, had it not been for the politeness for which I strive, and which never deserts me, I would have burst out laughing in the individual's face, so naïve did he seem. "I don't know," I said to him, in a slightly acerbic tone, "whether it is the custom in the country in which I have landed up—not of my own free will, I assure you—to greet strangers with tricks. To offer proof, however, of a courtesy that might perhaps set you an example, I shall answer your question. There are no longer any direct descendants of Louis XIV in France, and what's more, no one reigns over my country today."

My doctor opened his eyes wide in his turn. "No one reigns! Do you mean—pardon my retrospective and patriotic anguish—that France no longer exists?"

"Ha ha! That surpasses the bounds of permissible joking, Monsieur. France"—I emphasized the word by sitting up a little straighter—"exists, stronger, greater and more respected than ever."

"But the king…?"

"There is no longer a king."

"What? You say so? Isn't it you, Monsieur, who are playing games with my credulity in your turn? Who governs France, then?"

"No one…which is to say, everyone! Monsieur, we have the honor of being a republic!"

The doctor recoiled as if he had received a punch in the stomach. "A republic! But the Court of Versailles…of Saint-Germain…"

"There is no longer a court at Versailles or Saint-Germain, which are railway stations."

"What about the Bastille?"

"There is no Bastille any more…except for a railway station and a terminus for omnibuses and tramways.

The man seemed flabbergasted, thunderstruck.

I delivered the final blow. "Since it pleases you," I went on, "to interrogate me like a schoolboy, you will permit me to question you in my turn, and to summarize all my curiosity in two very simple formulas: who are you, and where am I?"

Then, quite simply, as if it were a matter of the most ordinary detail in the world, he replied: "My name is Durand, and you are in Paris."

"In Paris!" I cried, looking around.

The room in which I found myself, which I had scarcely had time to examine, could only be compared to a huge glass cage, but the windows were of a kind unknown to me, of which I could recall neither the nature nor the name, highly transparent but clearer and more solid in appearance than glass. The panes were retained by a lattice that was undoubtedly metallic, though not very shiny, and the whole assembly was supported, as I have said, by exceedingly slender colonnettes, which seemed scarcely solid enough, given their lightness, to sustain their burden.

The item of furniture—the bed—on which I was half-lying gave the sensation beneath my body of tightly stretched canvas, but when I put my hand on it, it felt much colder and much smoother than our linen. Whatever it was, however, the fabric was flexible enough to mold itself completely to the form of a body.

The rounded bed-frame was made of a shiny black material that was not reminiscent of ebony or black pearwood. That black color seemed, moreover, to be generally adopted by the furniture, for the room was equipped with several stools, a table and a dresser made of the same substance. All of it was formed with a singular character of antiquity. It seemed to me that I was in some museum of prehistoric things, whose origin I could not identify.

Numerous ideas crossed my mind. The man himself seemed almost to be a fossil; his complexion was dull, as if there were no life beneath the epidermis, and I recalled the bizarre impression that I had initially experienced at the sight of is garment, whose stiff folds were reminiscent of the cloaks of cathedral statues.

All of that caused me a profound emotion, a sort of anguish, and that unhealthy disposition doubtless showed in my face, for my doctor, swiftly drawing closer to me, said: "You're still in pain!"

"I don't know...and yet, yes, I'm very anxious..."

"Wait!" said the doctor. He went to the back of the room, where a frame was suspended, which bore some resemblance to a console of electric bells in a hotel. He pressed a switch and the light was suddenly modified; the windows—I can't call them anything else—changed color, becoming iridescent and opaline, emitting an infinitely gentler radiation, which enveloped me and penetrated me so pleasantly that my equilibrium was restored.

Then Monsieur Durand—since that was his name—went back to the console and put his finger on another button.

Several minutes went by during which I genuinely reveled in a delightful well-being. Then one of the panels opened, and I saw a creature that seemed to me to be gigantic: a bird with an enormous vulture-like head and extended wings, which was maintaining a kind of basket made of a grayish substance level with an external balcony.

Monsieur Durand took me by the hand and led me to the opening. He opened the basket at the side and ushered me into it. He got into it after me. The bird remained almost motionless, extending its vast wings over our heads, which were only making very gentle movements, doubtless designed to ensure its equilibrium in mid-air.

I gave up trying to reason and debate.

Monsieur Durand pronounced a word that I did not understand, then clicked his tongue. The bird began to glide through the air, carrying us away.

I looked down, and found that we were at an altitude of about a hundred meters—at least, that was my calculation, based on my previous ascents of the Eiffel Tower, how many hundreds of leagues away! I leaned over the edge of the basket and saw large buildings beneath me, separated from one another, within which and around which people were moving. Then there was a dark patch, which seemed to be an expanse of water.

Our progress was so rapid, however, that I did not have time for a more attentive examination—although I observed that the space through which the bird was flying was bounded on all sides by black rocks, rising up in places to prodigious heights, completing enclosing the horizon. It appeared to me to be about the size of the principality of Monaco.

I was snatched from these rapid calculations by the stopping of the bird, which had just deposited the basket, or gondola, on another balcony, formed by a large outcrop of rock, and I saw a large door in front of me on which was inscribed, in capital letters: GRAND CHATELET.[6]

---

[6] The original Grand Châtelet was the city prison of Paris for much of its existence, usually housing members of the lower classes, and had a horrid reputation; it was also the site of courts of justice in Old Paris. The edifice was finally destroyed in 1802. The Châtelet of modern Paris, like the other landmarks previously cited, is a railway station on the site of the Grand Châtelet, on the right bank of the Seine, opposite the Ile de la Cité, between the stations named for the Louvre and the Hôtel de Ville; the latter edifices still exist, although not in their original forms.

Monsieur Durand taking the lead, we stepped out on to the balcony and arrived at the said door.

V.

It was, no doubt, the entrance to an immense cave. It was six or eight meters in height, and opened into a large room that served as a vestibule.

Slight as my knowledge of mineralogy was, it was evident to me that the material in which the cavern was hollowed out belonged to the basalt family, black masses of which I had encountered astonishing specimens in my travels, at Cape Fairhead in Ireland—the Giants' Causeway—and in Fingal's Cave in the west of Scotland.

The ceiling of the vestibule was sustained by tall columns whose appearance was truly monumental. Daylight fully illuminated the walls, whose dark coloration was not at all sinister, for on prismatic arabesques had been carved into the surfaces of the walls, which brightened the play of the original light and were pleasant to behold.

At the appearance of Monsieur Durand, a man who was sitting in an armchair of near-white stone got up and came toward us with signs of evident respect. My guide muttered a few words in his ear and he immediately opened a door at the back of the vestibule and disappeared.

So far as I could see, the costume of the warden, usher or servant, was stiff and almost metallic in appearance, like that of the doctor, except that, instead of its long pleats falling the entire length of the body, it was adjusted in the form of a doublet by means of a golden belt. On his head he wore a hood, Medieval in form, and his legs disappeared into high boots.

I had decided not to question my guide any further; since every passing minute brought some new surprise, I deduced that I could only get lost in detailed interrogations that were rather foolish in themselves, and that it would be better, in order to obtain some enlightenment, to gather a certain umber of basic facts on which I could more usefully exercise the faculties of my intelligence. Besides, Doctor Durand seemed a trifle worried, and I had observed that at certain moments he darted glances at me that seemed to embody a kind of pity.

The rear door opened again. The warden bowed to Monsieur Durand and made a gesture inviting him to follow him.

"Will you wait here for me for a few moments," he said to me. "I will send someone to fetch you before long." Then, changing his mind, he said: "On second thoughts, it would be better for you to wait for me inside." He addressed himself to the warden: "Bernard, take Monsieur into the Denis Papin room."

Without waiting for my response, he left, while Monsieur Bernard opened a lateral door—the doors seemed to be made of sheets of slate—and showed me into a little room lit by electricity.

I use the word *electricity* because it corresponds exactly with the first impression that was imposed upon me, so clear and white was the light that enveloped me. Furthermore, the relevant apparatus bore a close resemblance to electric bulbs, save for the fact that the light, instead of being produced by an internal filament, emanated—at least so far as a rapid observation could inform me—from the entire surface of a little sphere. I had no idea whether the sphere was made of glass or metal, but all of its parts seemed to be animated by an incessant movement, so rapid that in trying to focus on them one was dazzled. The spheres were enveloped in a fine latticework, like lace or a web of silvery metal. At the same time—a very curious detail—I seemed to hear a sort of exceedingly subtle whistling sound, coming from a long way away, and somewhat muffled.

I did not have the leisure, however, to linger over lengthy observations, because there were so many surrounding objects soliciting my attention. On a pedestal that seemed to be made of porphyry, a rather poorly-executed bust was posed, which seemed nevertheless to be extraordinarily lifelike. It was the portrait of an old man with sunken, rather stunted features. At the base was a black plate, made of anthracite or pyrites, which bore a name: Denis Papin.

A little while before, when that name had been pronounced by Doctor Durand, I had thought I had misheard. Now, I could no longer be in any doubt; that room really did bear the name of the famous inventor of the autoclave, the first person to put steam to work. How did he come to be celebrated and honored in this part of the world, in this bizarre and mysterious place?

My hesitations, if any had remained, would soon have been dispelled, for I had before me, on a sort of stage carved out of basalt, a model of the famous digester, not made of cast iron but of stone. It was broken, as if it had burst, and the valve was no more than a scarcely-recognizable item of debris. In addition, on pieces of paper that were yellowed, as if corroded by time, I saw designs that had evidently been sketches of machines.

Continuing my investigation, I discovered yet more designs; these did not correspond to any of the notions that I possessed. They depicted a series of instruments in the form of trumpets, megaphones, harps, violas and rebecs; I could easily have believed them to be a collection of plans assembled by some amateur musician if these sound-making devices had not been connected by levers and crank-shafts to large cogwheels whose movement was indicated by curved arrows.

What relationship could there be between musical instruments and an engine for propagating movement?

So many ideas and hypotheses crossed my mind that I could not settle upon any of them, but I finally paused in front of a drawing that was larger than the others, representing a kind of boat above which clouds of smoke were escaping from a funnel, while oars plunged into the water. I remembered then that poor Papin had attempted—nearly two hundred years ago—experiments in steam navigation, and that his trial boat had been smashed by an ignorant mob...and that he had died in despair.

When had he died, in fact? At what date? I did not know.

As I was trying to remember, the door opened and Doctor Durand beckoned to me, with an anguished expression that unnerved me. "Come, Monsieur," he said. "Before deciding your fate, the High Court consents to hear you." He had pronounced these words in a tone so sad—lugubrious, even—that I began to shiver, without knowing why.

The cares that the doctor had lavished upon me, however, and the fact that I was an unfortunate and inoffensive individual, combined to convince me that I had nothing to fear. I followed the doctor. We went along a long corridor similarly lit by the strange bulbs, and I finally found myself in a vast room in which five judges were sat at an iron-legged table, while another magistrate was standing at a separate table.

The five judges—how, given their appearance, could I not call them by that name?—were, by some singular fantasy of historical reconstruction, costumed in the fashion of Louis XIV's time, draped in red robes trimmed with ermine, while their heads were buried in enormous wigs. Suddenly, I remembered having seen exactly the same men and the same costumes in a colored illustration representing a scene in the *Chambre Ardente*, under the great king, during the famous trial of la Voisin and la Filastre, the famous poisoners, whose prosecutor and instructing magistrate had been the Lieutenant of Police, La Reynie.[7]

Here the light was less bright, and the whistling sound that I had already perceived in the other room, still very soft, was lower in pitch, as if saddened. The overall impression was painful. I had not, however,

---

[7] The post of Lieutenant of Police was created by one of Louis XIV's ministers, Jean-Baptiste Colbert, as the first step in a slow process of bureaucratization that eventually produced modern police forces; its first holder was Gabriel Nicolas La Reynie (1625-1709), and the most famous *cause célèbre* in which he was involved was the "affair of the poisons," in which a relatively mundane case of poisoning became a virtual witch-hunt when suspicions of a wider conspiracy led him to round up and interrogate a number of fortune-tellers, one of whom—Catherine Dehayes Montvoisin, alias la Voisin—responded to pressure by inventing lurid tales of black masses attended by notable members of the court, including the king's mistress, Madame de Montespan. The *Chambre Ardente*—an extraordinary court summoned when needed to deal with politically sensitive cases in a quasi-inquisitorial fashion—took the initial denunciations seriously, but had to be reined in when the matter got seriously out of hand; the last person actually executed was Françoise Filastre, another fortune-teller.

committed any crime or misdemeanor; I therefore tried to suppress the emotion that took hold of me.

Doctor Durand stood next to me, and I heard him murmur these words, which did nothing to reassure me: "Be brave, Monsieur, be brave!"

What ordeals was I to undergo, then, which would require so much valor to endure?

I have said that the five judges were dressed in red; the sixth, who was standing, wore a black robe. In spite of my anxiety, which was very real, I noticed that all these garments were stiff, and that the fabric of which they were made was entirely unknown to me. This singular preoccupation left me ill-prepared for the extraordinary scene that was about to unfold.

The president—by which title I refer to the one who was sitting in the middle—fixed his eyes upon me and began to interrogate me.

"Do you swear to tell the truth, the whole truth…?"

"I so swear—but I should first like…"

"What is your name, forename, status and profession?"

"Alcide Trémalet, of no determined profession…"

"Where were you born?"

"In Paris."

"Paris…in France?"

I almost burst out laughing, but the magistrate's grave expression reminded me of the seriousness of the situation. "In France," I replied. "I do not know of any other."

"The prosecutor has the floor," the president went on, turning to the black-clad magistrate.

The prosecutor! This was becoming a bit much! I turned to Doctor Durand to call upon him as a witness to my perfect innocence. He had let his head fall into his hands, and his face was hidden.

"Gentlemen of the High Court," began the individual who had been designated by the terrible appellation *Prosecutor*, "it was a 120 years ago that your forefathers were called to pronounce judgment in a case absolutely identical case to the one brought before you today…"

"A 120 years ago, following an extraordinary accident, the exact nature of which has never been known, a man—a Frenchman—fell out of the sky from the clouds into our State. He claimed—as our archives testify—that he had risen up into the sky with the aid of a machine filled with air, which, he affirmed, had been drawn through the atmosphere under the impulsion of the wind; that the aforementioned machine had burst, and that he had been thrown from a prodigious height to the ground.

"I shall remind you succinctly of the circumstance to which he owed his salvation; at that time, our ancestors were engaged in their first experiments with the parason, and networks of remarkable fineness and resilience had been extended over our city—which was then, as you know, much smaller. The mesh of the parason had deadened the stranger's fall. He was brought before you, after having received the cares that his condition necessitated, and he was interrogated.

"We possess the written record of that remarkable hearing, in which those whose seats you occupy today decided that the security of the State, superior to any other consideration, required the death of the man whom ill fortune had thrown into our midst.

"I must remind you of the arguments that dictated the decision in question.

"In the wake of the terrible events that drove our forefathers from their fatherland, when they were obliged to flee the worst kinds of persecution, after a cosmic catastrophe that enclosed them in the basalt ring in which we still live today, it took nearly a century for the society they formed, which was then not very numerous, to acquire—at the cost of great effort and enormous travails—the tranquility and well-being to which they had the right, the first condition of which was the isolation that they had valiantly accepted, and which was the guarantee of their present and future security.

"Our forefathers had sworn that relations would never be re-established between themselves and the people that had inflicted so much bitterness and pain upon them. What they wanted, and what they demanded, was to be forgotten. Resigned to know nothing of other human beings, they were determined to remain unknown to them—but now a representative of the race of persecutors had suddenly come among them; he had stumbled across the secret of our existence unwittingly, he said—but what guarantee did we have of his sincerity? What proof did we have that he was not an emissary sent by our former proscribers? What guarantee did we have, if we spared his life, that he was not in possession of some unknown means of escaping our enclosure—by taking the aerial route again, for example?

"Then he would return to his homeland, to the world of men. He would betray us, he would denounce us, and we—who had renounced everything in order to preserve our independence, who had consented to all sacrifices in order to create a happy existence for ourselves, sheltered from all peril—would see cruel and ignorant men invading our refuge, bringing machines of war to open breaches in our rocks, taking possession of our children and our wives…as before!

"No, we had a duty to ourselves, to protect ourselves and our people by removing even the possibility of such a catastrophe...

"That, gentlemen of the High Court, is what the man who occupied my position said to the men who occupied yours...and your forefathers, gentlemen, did not hesitate. They remembered the fine Roman maxim that the safety of the people is the first law, and the stranger—whose name it is unnecessary to recall here—was condemned to death.

"To be sure, the execution of that sentence was an occasion of mourning for our Republic, but only a few protests were raised. That was, as we remember even after 120 years, the first—and, until now, only—decisive scientific application of the Phonothanatos."

At this point the individual raised his arms above his head. "Perhaps, however, 100 years hence, the magistrate who will take my place, before your successors, will recall a second example of your justice. He will say that, for a second time, the salvation of the Republic demanded a terrible but inevitable sentence from you...

"Whatever explanations this man might be able to offer, they cannot prevail against this fact: he has introduced himself into our State without our consent. Has he come to spy on us, as a secret agent? That is a secret that will remain between him and his conscience—but what is beyond any doubt is that from this moment on, he is the master of our fate. We must not take account either of the protestations of good faith that he will undoubtedly lavish upon us, or the promises that he will not fail to make that he will never escape from here and never reveal our existence. I say that he cannot offer us any real and indubitable guarantee, that his existence is not a threat permanently suspended over the city that we have called Paris—in memory of the old capital from which we were driven out—and which our poets, in their prescient anticipation of the future, have called Mysteryville!

"Yes, we live in Mysteryville, and it is necessary that mystery should continue to envelop us forever...

"I conclude: this man is, or will be, a public enemy.

"I demand that he be subjected to the punishment of the Phonothanatos."

I had listened to this furious speech with wide open eyes and a haggard expression. What did it all mean? What were these allusions to a past of which I was ignorant, to persecutions of which I had certainly not been the author or an accomplice?

Guilty? Me? Of what misdeed? Why these suspicions of espionage and treason? Why demand that I be subjected to some unknown punishment with a bizarre name, which concealed death—perhaps horrible and agonizing—beneath its hypocritical syllables?

I had experienced such a shock that a surge of rage made me cry out: "You are either the greatest of imbeciles or the most ferocious of executioners!"

The Prosecutor did not move, as if the invective had not reached his ears. The president leaned toward his assistants, exchanged a few whispered words, and then—finally—addressed himself to me. "Have you any observations to make?"

"Any observations!" I cried. "Much more than that! I have to declare that all of that man's arguments are monstrous, more than inhuman, and unworthy of a sane person!"

"Explain yourself calmly," the president said.

At the same time, my introducer, Doctor Durand, tugged at my clothing, evidently by way of urging me charitably to moderation.

"So be it," I said. "I shall try to restrain my indignation—but is it not odious that the mere fact of having suffered misfortune, of being separated from one's fatherland and one's people, should constitute in your eyes a crime worthy of the ultimate punishment?"

And, raising myself up to the highest eloquence (you will forgive me that slight impulse of vanity), I brought out all the inhumanity of that speech, which lacked the most elementary basis—which is to say, any real criminality.

With perfect frankness, I told the story of my horrible adventure. I described my sojourn in rural China, the suddenness of the attack directed against my life, the logic of my flight and, at the same time, the unconsciousness into which a perfectly natural terror had thrown me. Did I even know in which direction that panic-stricken flight had taken me? Was I responsible for my pathological state of mind, provoked by a cause entirely independent of my will?

Then, finally, I had arrived, without knowing how or why, in a sort of exit-less gorge. I emphasized that point: exit-less! Had I been left to my own devices, it was certain that I would never have been able to scale an utterly inaccessible rock. Who had hoisted me up to the summit of that inaccessible wall? That serpent, that monster, had grabbed me—where had it come from, if not from among those who were now setting themselves up as judges and intending to punish me—for what? For having been the victim of one of the disgusting creatures that they ought to have destroyed?

At that part of my argument, the logic of which gave me every satisfaction, I seemed to see a smile pass over the lips of the tribunal members. I sensed that I was getting somewhere, and I continued more forcibly.

"Thus, I have established in the most peremptory fashion that I did not come here of my own free will, and that is the very people who brought me into their country, via the intermediary of a hideous monster, who are now reproaching me for being here. Does that make sense? Is that equitable?" I paused, then continued with a new vigor: "No, you will not convict an innocent man. And besides, what are the odious suspicions that you are entertaining really worth?

"What do you have to fear from me? That I might betray you? How, and why? How? You are surrounded by inaccessible walls, and any escape seems impossible to me. But why should I escape? Am I thinking about it? I'm curious, it's true—extremely curious—but after having traveled the world and having found nothing there but banality and repetition, I have the good fortune finally to arrive in a region where everything seems new, amazing and inexplicable...would I even think about returning to the world of wearying familiarity that I left of my own free will? Get away! You don't know me at all.

"Betray you? Draw the attention of the world to you? Why would I do that? Even if I were capable of such baseness, what good would it do me? What benefit would I obtain from it? Besides, gentlemen, you only have to bind me to you forever by gratitude. Enchain me by your generosity and your benevolence, and I will remain with you until I die, demanding only to be your most humble and devoted servant: signed, Alcide Trémalet."

I pronounced those final words in a rather light one, to the extent that, in listening to myself, I was convinced of the success of my case.

Then the Prosecutor got up and said: "Having heard the case and having heard the accused, I persist in my demand, to which may it please the tribunal to address itself directly."

On the injunction of that man—who evidently lacked both heart and reason—the tribunal seemed to deliberate and I heard, as if through a fog, as if in a nightmare, the sentence that condemned me…to the Phonothanatos!

Uttering a cry of despair, I fainted into Doctor Durand's arms.

VI.

Phonothanatos can be broken down into "phono," which signifies sound, vocal or musical, and "thanatos," which signifies death. The latter part was perfectly clear—but the former made me think.

What could the exact relationship between the two terms be?

The doctor had taken me back to the Denis Papin room and had there put me back in the hands of the usher who had met us on our arrival. The latter had taken me through the vestibule when a voice called out: "Bring forward Monsieur le President's vulture!" And I had seen my horrible judge climb into a basket almost identical to the one that had brought me and disappear into the sky, carried off by an enormous vulture. Then a condor had come, bearing an even larger gondola—a sort of omnibus—in which the other judges had taken their places.

I remained alone with the warden, Bernard, who introduced me into a dark and ominous cell, where he abandoned me before I could question him, noisily closing an exceedingly heavy door behind him, which separated me from the living world.

My strength was exhausted, and I was literally dying of hunger. In a fit of rage, I hurled myself upon the door as if I might be able to break it down, howling and yelling, lavishing insults jupon my executioners.

The door opened again, and Doctor Durand came in. The warden was with him, bearing various rounded flasks with long, thin necks, equipped with taps. The idea crossed my mind that these were instruments of torture and that I was about to be subjected to intolerable torments, like those inflicted in ancient times by High Courts upon the unfortunates, innocent or not, whom they wished to force to confess to their crimes.

Bernard brought out a table and placed the bizarre flasks on it. Then, in response to a sign, he left, and once again I found myself alone with the doctor.

The latter pressed a switch on the wall and a bulb had lit up, with a sound so shrill that I feared it might rupture my eardrum, but he quickly regulated what was presumably the escape of the gas—was it a gas?—and the sound had softened to the point of being scarcely perceptible. "Did you call out?" he asked me.

"I'm hungry?" I told him.

"I assumed that you would be," he replied, "so I had a fortifying meal rapidly prepared for you. I won't try to hide it from you—you'll need all your strength."

I opened my mouth to protest again, and to interrogate him.

"Don't think about what's going to happen," said Durand. "Eat first."

"Eat what?" I asked, indicating the table. "I'm not accustomed to nourishing myself with stone or metal."

"This is the menu," said Durand, gravely. "Braised beef and carrots, seasoned with veal sauce, Pont-Lévêque cheese…"

"What? What sort of joke is this? Where's the food? Do you think naming it will suffice to satisfy my stomach?"

"I didn't have time to consult you as to what wine you prefer. You'll find an excellent Ile-de-France there..."[8]

Enough!" I cried. "Have I fallen into the midst of ferocious madmen? Before killing me, are they determined to drive me mad too?"

"Now, now!" said Durand. "Don't get carried away. I greatly regret the sentence passed on you by the High Court, which will be carried out in two hours..."

"What? What did you say?"

"I said that the sentence passed upon you by the Supreme Court will be carried out in 120 minutes..."

"But that sentence is infamous, monstrous...I appeal to you, who have cared for me—I'm damned if I know how! To kill me without my having committed any crime...!"

"It is, indeed revolting," said the excellent Doctor Durand, in the calmest possible tone, "but what can you do about it? Any debate would be futile. You're going to die—unjustly, but you won't be any less dead."

"And I can't even appeal against this iniquitous sentence?"

"There's no provision for that. Although, you know, your particular case is the only one that goes to the High Court. Don't judge our justice by that example. On the contrary, we have the most equitable tribunals..."

---

[8] The Ile-de-France in question is the one in the river Oise, not the one that subsequently became known as Mauritius, as is made clear when it is given the alternative name of Argenteuil. Now swallowed by up by Parisian sprawl, the locality once produced what was, in effect, the city's "local wine," which would be treasured on that account by the nostalgic Mystery-villains.

"What does the equity of the others matter to me, if the injustice of this one has cost me my life?"

Doctor Durand clapped me on the shoulder paternally. "Come on! What good does it do to excite yourself like this? You don't have to convince me—I know that you're perfectly innocent, and I will apply to the sentence that has been passed on you all the epithets of blame that you might care to choose. That won't prevent you from dying in two hours....or from being hungry. The best thing to do is to take your last meal with me, with as much gaiety as possible."

Don't forget that I had nothing in front of me but flasks or alembics, the appearance of which had nothing culinary about it. My bewilderment cut off my speech—perhaps in combination with the certainty of an all-too-imminent denouement—but Durand went on: "Let me handle this—put your trust in me. By the way, do you eat bread?"

"Certainly, when I'm in a human land..."

He drew closer to the table, examined the flasks, and grouped them in unequal numbers. "Ah, here's the bread!" he said. "It might seem a little stale to you. We don't eat it often, and the central factory only makes it twice a week."

I had given up protesting. I regarded everything as the substance of a nightmare. With the most perfect composure in the world, however, Durand took a little flexible tube from the table, tipped with—how shall I put this?—a cigarette-holder of the amber variety, and deliberately set it between my lips. Then he connected it to one of the flasks and turned the little tap—and a delicious mouthful of beef and carrots expanded in my mouth.

The doctor closed the tap, put another amber nozzle into my mouth, and I received the gustatory impression of a very good bread...perhaps a trifle overcooked.

The illusion—for it could only an illusion—was such that my jaws carried out the chewing movements of their own accord. In truth, I ate, I swallowed—and, instinct suddenly taking over, I put the beef cannula and the bread cannula alternately to my mouth (after all, cannula, so the dictionary assures me, means "little reed") and I savored them slowly, finding the choice meat and vegetables excellent.

"A drop of wine!" said Doctor Durand.

I looked around—fruitlessly—for a glass, but my host obligingly showed me another little reed, from which I breathed in. A sensation of wine dilated my palate, against which my tongue clicked gratefully.

Needless to say—isn't it?—no solid or liquid had touched my taste buds; the physical impression was of a kind of gas: a fluid that gave the exact impression of genuine ingurgitation. "That's astonishing!" I cried, taking hold of the wine reed again, passionately.

"Not so fast," said Durand, smiling. "That little Ile-de-France, which is also known as Argenteuil, and which old king Henri IV held in high esteem, is sometimes a little perfidious..."

"But after all," I exclaimed, "I beg you, Maître Durand, to tell me whether I'm asleep or awake! Everything I see, everything I hear, everything that surrounds me appears to me to be to be fake and phantasmal. It's grotesque and tragic at the same time. Have pity on my poor brain—and for the little time that it has left to exercise its faculties, don't subject it to the exhausting work of questioning the incomprehensible. What is all this? Am I really on Earth, or on some other sublunary planet?"

"I'd certainly like to furnish you with a few explanations," he said, "for your emotion doesn't surprise me at all. Promise me at least to remain calm and eat peacefully while I edify you with regard to what you want to know…"

"I promise you that I won't even interrupt you."

"Anyway, here's something to occupy your mind." He drew another flask toward him and fixed a gustatory tube to it. "This is a game pâté—hare and pheasant—about which you'll give me your opinion."

"What! You have hares and pheasants here, in the middle of the Gobi desert?"

"You promised to let me speak. Content yourself with enjoying gastronomic pleasures for the last time—and listen to me…"

Those words recalled me to reality for the last time and persuaded me to keep silent—and I attacked the imaginary pâté, which I washed down conscientiously with non-existent Argenteuil wine.

Durand leaned against the wall, and spoke to me thus: "Since you're French, you'll know the history of your country, and won't be unaware that on the eighteenth of October 1685…"

"The revocation of the Edict of Nantes!" I exclaimed.

"Indeed—it was on that date that King Louis XIV made the terrible and cruel error of expelling from France the most devoted and most active of his subjects. But let's not recriminate. The fact must be recalled because it's the point of departure of our story. The inhabitants of New Paris, where you are at present—or Mysteryville—are the descendants of a group of French exiles, Parisians to be precise, driven out by a law that confirmed and aggravated the definitive Act of which we speak.

"Having been brought up in France, you will recall better than our learned men the dolorous circumstances of that exodus. For, after the terrible events that led us into the desert where we are, you will understand that our ancestors did not take much account at first of past events—to the extent that we know almost nothing about the catastrophe of which we were the victims. All that we know for certain is that shortly after the year 1700, a significant company of our ancestors found themselves in Germany, in Kassel or Marburg, and that there was among them there a man of genius, persecuted, unfortunate and destitute, who was named Denis Papin."

"The true inventor of the steam engine; the man whose ideas have transformed the world!"

"I don't know what transformation of the world you're alluding to," Durand went on. "The ideas of Denis Papin have always remained quite obscure to us, and the role that you attribute to steam is incomprehensible to us."

"But in the room that bears his name I saw the sketch of the steam-boat, whose conception was genius…!"

"You promised me not to interrupt," the Doctor said. "You're forgetting that time is passing and we're getting closer to the moment…"

"Of the Phonothanatos!" I said, in an ironic tone. "Indeed, I thank you for having reminded me of that detail. Continue, I beg you." The fact is that Doctor Durand's response had chilled my curiosity—but he paid no heed to my impatience.

"I mentioned Denis Papin," he continued. "What we know for sure about him is that he did, indeed, attempt to solve an interesting problem—navigation by the force of heated water—that was, like us, forbidden. With us, he had constructed a boat of which he made a trial on a German river, and which the boatmen had smashed up.

"Since that time he had lived in poverty, despairing and half-mad. It was then that he met a group of Frenchmen who, having pooled all their resources, were planning to leave inhospitable Europe and go to seek their fortune in some unexplored country. This happened in the early years of the eighteenth century.

"It appears that, gathering together the last debris of their former wealth, our forefathers furnished Denis Papin with the means to make another attempt to construct his boat, and that the work was completed in a European port, the name of which we don't know, but which must have been in England. As to how many exiles embarked on that vessel with him, we have never been able to determine the exact number.

"What were the vicissitudes of that voyage? By what waves was the mysterious vessel pitched and tossed? Our archives are mute in that regard. Of matters that date from nearly two hundred years ago, we are reduced to conserving traditions that lack any precision. Evidently, Denis Papin's vessel became the plaything of tides and tempests, went around Africa and set forth at hazard across the Indian Ocean. Finally, it was wrecked on the eastern shore of India.

"Then began a pilgrimage of unspeakable pain and fatigue, amid fanatical peoples. Our unfortunate ancestors, who were fleeing persecution, found it again, even more ardent and more ferocious than before, among the fanatical hordes of the worshippers of Siva. Certain names have remained in our memory, with surges of terror: the Punjab, Lahore, Srinagar, Kashmir, the pass of

Karakorum…there they succeeded in founding a colony of sorts, and finding themselves sheltered from any further peril. Then there was one last massacre, and a hectic flight through the desert—evidently between Turkestan and China—and then the final cataclysm, which ought to have completed the destruction of our forefathers forever.

"What was that upheaval? The incoherent stories that have reached us via the oral tradition that is transmitted from mouth to mouth, permit us to attribute it to a sudden volcanic eruption. Our forefathers and their wives—who had constituted, since the Indian coast, a veritable tribe lost in the desert, a group of families deprived of everything, marked for death—were, therefore, newcomers in an entirely unknown territory, where there was no longer any trace of human habitation.

"That solitude was a relief and consolation in itself; at least the fugitives no longer heard clamors of hatred ringing in their ears, and were no longer agitated by shudders of terror. It was a march toward death, but without any dolorous struggle against fellow men, against individuals who ought to have merited the title of brothers but had only revealed themselves as executioners.

"Meanwhile, no help being any longer expected, the unfortunates—all of whose supplies were exhausted—resigned themselves to their frightful death. They gathered together for one last time in order to exchange a final farewell, and then lay down on the ground, knowing that half of them would probably not wake up the following day.

"Suddenly, in the middle of the night, there was a frightful convulsion. The ground trembled, opened up, and vomited forth torrents of lava. At the same time, in the sky, livid lightning-flashes were the prelude to the unleashing of thunderbolts. Here, our imagination can be given free rein to create a formidable picture of that commotion which shook the earth to its most profound depths. Nothing could have been more sinister than that scene of desolation, in which people were struggling who were scarcely capable of resistance, whose strength had been exhausted by privations, and among whose agonizing mass there were women and children!

"Now, according to the more-or-less exact indications that we have been able to gather regarding that frightful convulsion of nature, it seems evident that a sort of lava volcano had suddenly erupted in the middle of the desert and that, by some caprice of the blind forces of matter, it had formed a near-circular basaltic wall all around the place in which our ancestors had ended up, imprisoning them in a completely sealed enclosure—a frightful barrier that separated them forever from the human species.

"How many people survived that horrible commotion? It has been impossible for us to establish any statistic on that subject. Those few groups of survivors, relegated to a terrain made of black rock, which formed a single mass in which it seemed that no tool could make a dent, must have experienced such fits of despair that we can now understand the oath of hatred then sworn by the survivors against the people who had reduced them to that terrible extremity. Deprived of all resources, without provisions and without instruments, they were immured, without any hope of escape—and yet, they did not admit defeat."

Durand paused, and then went on: "They were a strong and courageous race, of whom we are honored to be the descendants, but to whom we also owe our desire for isolation, our unbreakable resolution never to enter into communication with the rest of the world. In the two centuries that have elapsed since then, it has been necessary to create a new civilization from scratch, to invent a technology and an industry, to discern which of the forces of nature we would be able to utilize...oh, how slow our progress was! There was no vegetation in our prison save for miserable lichens and scarce ferns. There was no water, and no springs, except for a lake a few meters wide in the middle of a terrain composed of schist and slate—a bottomless gulf from which all animal life was absent, and seemed fated to remain so for ever more.

"The excess of our misfortune was also our salvation; the very sky, in seeming to be our enemy, snatched us from the jaws of death, for it was from the sky that enormous birds came: vultures and condors, monsters of the air, which, having identified their human prey, fell upon those exhausted individuals in order to devour them. It must have been an atrocious battle, equal to the most sinister battles of barbaric times.

"Our fathers were victorious; not only did they kill those hideous enemies, but they actually captured a few pairs alive. The flesh of the dead served them as nourishment and they reduced the others to a state of slavery. You have seen yourself that these animals, domesticated and tamed, now serve as a means of transport, and that their docility is only equaled by the precision and mildness of their service."

Durand paused again, and then concluded: "I thought that I ought to give you these explanations. I profoundly regret that the sentence passed on you prevents me from giving you more details of the prodigies that we have achieved..."

"And I regret it even more than you do!" I cried. "For in all of this I see nothing that justifies the cruelty with which those men, born of the same race as myself and in whose veins flows the same blood as mine, are treating an unfortunate who has, like them, been the victim of the wickedness of others. Just answer me this simple question: was it of my own volition that I came among you?"

"No, I admit that. And on that subject, I can still give you some further information. We have explored the enclosure which, in imprisoning us forever, protects us from contact with and the violence of men. We know that on the far side of the rocks that surround us there are a few fissures, gullies that might perhaps communicate with the external world by means of subterranean tunnels that we have not yet been able to discover. It was doubtless through one of these unknown tunnels that you penetrated into the crevasse in which you were trapped, as if in a corridor with no exit.

"For a long time now, we have maintained a system of surveillance; the slightest sound produced in the fissures in the rock is communicated to us, thanks to means of the amplification of sound that we have invented, with great rapidity and perfect precision. Thus, we knew that some animal, perhaps a human being, was wandering in our interior barrier, and we therefore deployed our pneumatic aspirator…"

"What? That repulsively ugly entity that resembles a serpent…"

"Was merely the hose-pipe of our aspiratory machine, powered, like all our machines, by sound. Its force is such that within a radius of 80 meters it draws in, swallows up and consumes all the objects in its range. You could not escape it. You were seized, and lifted up.

At first, you were in a state of exhaustion that made me fear for your life. I shut you up in the photophonic glass-house of the Hôpital Saint-Martin, which is the room where we carry out medical treatment by means of light, music and perfume, and you recovered.

"My duty then was to take you before the High Court, which I did. I hoped, I confess, that our great judges would show indulgence in your regard. They did not. Once again, I am heartbroken, for I like you…"

I interrupted him with bitter laughter. "What would have happened, then, if you had not liked me? Your great judges are the born conservers of ancient customs."

"Our great judges are charged with watching over the security of our colony. They have conserved the most absolute respect for the decisions of our ancestors. A hundred years ago, as you have been told, a man introduced himself among us and was put to death. That is the only instance in our legislation in which that punishment—preservative of our independence—can be applied. I have no argument with you as to whether it might seem just or unjust. Our great judges have only conformed to centuries-old tradition…"

"Which is to say that I'm the victim of the most odious kind of fanaticism. So be it. It's just as well that I shall not return to the company of civilized men, for, on my honor, I would hasten to denounce this den of cannibals to universal indignation."

"I cannot permit you the crime," my excellent doctor interrupted, "of railing in anger against a custom that is evidently prejudicial to you. Once again, have I not taken the trouble to prove to you that we are not cannibals? For my part, I deplore this stubbornness in outdated customs—but it seems to me that in your country, so long as a law has not been repealed…"

This reasoning had little impact on me. Did he, perhaps, imagine that I would end up approving of the iniquity that would cost me my life? But one last item of curiosity gripped me. "Would you at least deign to explain to me what the Phonothanatos is?"

"With pleasure," he replied, politely. It is, as the Hellenic origin of the word indicates, death by sound…"

"I don't understand."

"Well, in circumstances that I can't reveal to you, our forefathers, about 120 years ago, established that sound possessed an extraordinary ability to disorganize atoms. Aren't you aware, Monsieur, that sometimes, in cathedrals, windows have been seen to break in response to a note sounded by the organ?"

"That's true. I've even heard of a violinist who, on the emission of a note that was not even very loud, broke the windows of a room…"

"That's the same thing. We have studied sound intensively, Monsieur, and we draw the greater part of the motive force that we require therefrom. Its vibrations have been regulated and channeled, in various ways, by us. Sound is the basis of our technology, our industry, even our therapeutics. Its physiological effects are extraordinary." He lowered his voice, and added: "And they're sometimes astonishingly murderous. Thus, I repeat: the Phonothanatos is execution by sound—but you're about to be informed of that at first-hand…"

Indeed, footsteps could be heard in a neighboring room, drawing nearer. The door opened and I saw, in the midst of the great judges who had come to witness the execution of their sentence…a young woman, delightfully pretty, with eyes of a celestial purity, who was holding a musical instrument reminiscent in its form of an antique cithara.[9] She was dressed in white, as if in a sheath of marble or alabaster. One might have thought her an exquisite Greek statue descended from her pedestal; she reminded me of some allegorical nymph in the bowers of Versailles—and, involuntarily, I admired that creature of dreams...

She looked at me sadly. The great judges installed themselves on stools surrounding me; Doctor Durand took up a position to my right.

The young deity stood facing me, her bow raised...

I noticed—and I was convinced that it would be the last observation of my life—that the great judges and the young woman had their heads covered by a sort of cap made of a very fine mesh, like silver filigree, held in place like a hair-net, hermetically enveloping the skull and the ears. Doctor Durand too had rigged himself out in a helmet of that sort—whose purpose, I confess, I did not seek to understand. I had other things to worry about, for I now had no doubt that my last hour had come...and even though I had grasped very little from the vague explanation of the operation of the Phonothanatos, I could not prevent myself from suffering a dolorous anguish as I anticipated its effects...

The young musician half-closed her eyes. Holding the cithara in her slightly curved left arm, she placed the bow on the strings....

Then there was the sweetest sensation that I had ever experienced; carelessly, I let my own eyelids fall, in order that no impression might disturb the intoxicating pleasure that delighted my ears and penetrated my brain. It was a complete well-being, with an artistic joy that no words can express; the sound seemed to me to realize,

---

[9] A kind of lyre with a wooden case.

by means of combinations of chords unknown to me—which I had not observed in the works of Beethoven, Wagner, or even Debussy—the evocation of harmonies never heard before. And all those notes were made, I knew, of vibrations that were linking together, blending, unifying and, by the gradations of an astonishing science, gradually developing in me an auditory aptitude with which I was unfamiliar...

With one phrase I can make myself understood: it was a terrifying exquisiteness, in the sense that, little by little, I felt that all the fibers of my being were being stretched further and further, that the maximum of life was being realized in me, and that I was attaining the supreme limit of human delectation...

I opened my eyes again, and the people and objects before me appeared in a vaporous iridescence, through which all the nuances of the prism passed, sometimes slow and sometimes fulgurant: a scintillating irradiation that dazzled me. And I felt that death was about to arrive. Yes, it's very strange, but my ears expected, and somehow yearned for, the note whose vibration, adapted to that of my cerebral lobes, would provoke disorganization while transporting me into the vortex of melodious spheres...

Yes, it was putting an end to me. I was undergoing annihilation. I was dissolving in harmony...when, all of a sudden, a loud clamor of shouting and thumping on the door of my prison ripped through the veil of euphony in which I was enveloped.

It was an abrupt, almost painful awakening.

The door of my prison flew upon in response to a violent effort, and I saw a flood of children, between eight and 12 years old, coming in, rosy with youth—who, grabbing hold of the great judges, addressed vehement words to them that my still-languid hearing had difficulty in seizing…

Doctor Durand, leaning toward my ear, said: "It had to happen one day. It's the Revolution!"

I witnessed a very curious scene, and I shall try to share with those who might read these lines the profound emotion that it caused me.

I don't know exactly how we returned to the courtroom in which I had earlier been tried and condemned, but this time it was the judges in red robes and Louis XIV wigs who were in the dock; it was the prosecutor who was guarded by the warden, Bernard, and was looking around anxiously. And sitting in tribunal were 20 young people—I should rather say children—clad in blouses and wearing large white collars: a uniform almost exactly similar to that of our Sunday school pupils. One of them occupied the president's chair. He was certainly not the oldest, being scarcely ten or 12, while I noticed others who must have been 15 or 16.

A great hubbub was audible outside; I later found out that, with a purpose that will be explained, schoolchildren had taken possession of all the transport company's condors and vultures, and that they were being transported in convoy[10] to the Grand Châtelet—which had resulted in the unexpected invasion of all those young people, a great many of whom were still outside on the exterior terrace. The transporter birds had been

---

[10] There is a pun here that defies translation; where I have simply written "transported in convoy," Lermina has "*convoyer—or convoler.*".The literal meaning of *convoler* is "to remarry" but it includes *voler* [to fly] and thus looks as if it perhaps ought to mean "to convey by air," as opposed to "to proceed in convoy," that being the literal meaning of *convoyer*.

retained, and by virtue of that, all communication had been cut between the city below and the Grand Châte-let—where the storm of revolution was, as will be seen, about to burst.

VII.

When I was introduced, the president of the young people—a handsome boy with a lofty forehead and a frank gaze—got to his feet and bowed to me.

The gesture was so unexpected, so distant in character from the habits of judges in my own land that, in surprise, I turned round to look behind me for the privileged mortal to whom it might be addressed.

"Man," said the president then, in a clear and pleasant voice, "know that you are free and that, if you express the desire, you will be immediately conducted out of this enclosure, to wherever you may please. It is, therefore, in the capacity of temporary guest, and not that of an accused person, that we pray you now to answer our questions."

The old judges stirred, giving unequivocal signs of impatient protest, but the group of children charged with their surveillance held them more tightly, forcing them to remain still.

In the meantime, having recovered my self-composure—although I still had a certain musical buzz in my ears—I explained myself very calmly, relating in terms of a courtesy equal to that which I had been shown the vicissitudes of my recent adventure: the nocturnal attack of the Chinese, my hectic flight, and, finally, my involuntary penetration into the territory of the unknown city.

The president listened to me with rapt attention.

That tribunal, in which only fresh and rosy faces could be seen, was a truly original affair. Some of the kids still had baby faces, and were contemplating me with lovely large eyes, others with sly and slightly mocking expressions.

"I cannot, therefore, admit," I said, as I finished, "that I should suffer the worst of punishments, without having committed any real misdemeanor, and since I am permitted to protest against the iniquitous sentence imposed upon me, I make that appeal as forcefully as I can, to good faith and justice."

"And you are right!" the president said to me. Then he turned to the great judge who had directed the hearing that had terminated so badly for me a little while before. "Grandfather," he said, "Will you answer my questions…?"

The man thus addressed, however, had raised himself up to his full height and, rolling up the sleeves of his red robe over his forearms—parenthetically, that singular cloth folded back in the fashion of the little screens of Japanese furniture—he cried: "What is this? By what right do urchins of your sort permit themselves to intervene in the high justice of which we are the dispensers? Do you think that we shall permit this strike—which is both insolent and grotesque—against the authority in which we are vested? Be fearful of the terrible whipping that will punish your ridiculous indiscretion!"

"You're forgetting," the president interrupted, "that all corporal punishment has been suppressed by the law of year 163; moreover, I shall explain to you, venerable grandfather, by what right we are intervening and why we are here."

"I'm curious to hear your arguments. That might still afford us some amusement." The great judges sniggered.

Very calmly, however, the little judge continued; "You are not unaware of the profound reforms that our great Jean Martin 88..."

Here I need to open a parenthesis. You will observe that all the inhabitants of this country bear eminently French names such as Durand, Dupont, Martin, Bernard, Dupin, Meunier, Legros, Leblanc, Lebrun, etc., etc.— evident proof of their origin—but the number of these similar appellations was such that it was necessary to distinguish them by means of numerals. There was a Dupont 31 and a Duval 333.

So, as the little judge was saying: "...the profound reforms that our great Jean Martin 88 introduced into our education system. Before him, that education was both despotic and mnemotechnic. He thought of rendering it amicable and rational.

"I will not remind you of the struggles that it was necessary to sustain against the partisans of the former doctrines, against those fanatics of recitation who gave prizes to any pupil who had repeated 500 consecutive words without understanding a single one, but with mechanical precision. Jean Martin 88 declared in his revolutionary program that not a single word would henceforth be pronounced by a child without his knowing exactly what it meant, without his being able to paraphrase in another clear and explanatory form any sentence that his memory suggested to him.

"It was a total revolution; the masters who had until then been nothing but pedagogues soon became the awakeners of intellects. That which had been decorated with so many big words—philosophy, logic, Aristotelianism, Cartesianism, Platonism—was transformed into a single science, that of common sense and justice.

"You will recall the most admirable innovation of that father of our consciences. He imagined continually setting children up as judges, routinely putting to them questions of good and evil, calling upon them to offer their opinions on matters great and small, on the merits and demerits of their comrades and themselves. The ridiculous exercises of scholasticism—whose traditions our forefathers had unfortunately preserved—gave way to a kind of gymnastics of equality.

"Do you remember this admirable speech by Jean Martin 88? 'Just as a child, having learned with the greatest difficulty to walk and to read, gradually succeeds in carrying out these various actions without even thinking about them, as habitual actions that no longer require effort, it is similarly necessary that a moral gymnastics arduously and carefully executed should accustom the lobes of his brain to equity, that his cerebral fibers should gradually acquire such a habitude, in order that later in life, the realization of justice will be, in a sense, independent of his will, any injustice automatically provoking a resistance of equity, and any blameworthy act leading, as if by a mechanical trigger, to protest and reparation.'

"Jean Martin 88 continued: "Thus, just as an eyelid closes by virtue of an involuntary contraction as soon as there is a threat to the eye, so the conscience, as soon as there is any threat to the good and the just, will, so to speak, bristle, by virtue of a reflex action, in order to create an obstacle to it and repel it.'

"It is according to these principles that, thanks to the efforts of the League for the Spontaneity of Justice, we have been brought up. Over several generations, the effect of this education has been such that neither crimes not misdemeanors any longer exist among us, and that even the paltry arguments of vanity, personal interest and ill-intentioned self-regard have almost completely disappeared.

"Combative tribunals have been suppressed, or at least no longer find any occasion to function; conciliatory judges, benevolent arbiters, suffice for all matters, and you are aware that quite recently, the law has inflicted official sanctions on judges who cannot succeed in conciliating a litigation. In consequence, the organization of social and economic life in our country has taken on a confidence and mutual solidarity that will soon achieve perfection. Little by little, all outdated, egotistical ideas—which make men wolves for other men—are being erased.

"However, it there still remains what I am pleased to call one sanctuary of privilege and routine, like a conservatory of irrationality and barbarism. I tell you this forthrightly: it is the High Court!"

"We will not tolerate this outage of a centuries-old institution!" cried the great judge.

"Which is in the wrong precisely by virtue of being two hundred years old!" cried the little judge. "Times, methods and people change. Institutions must change too."

"We have a responsibility to public safety…"

"You had that responsibility when the memory of ancient persecutions displayed that security as perpetually under threat. Then, justice was veiled by fear. Today, the education that we have received has borne fruit, and when we, the children of truth and equity, learned that, by virtue of ancient customs, the life of an innocent man was in peril, a force superior to our own will, that reflex of virtue that the education of Jean Martin 88 has developed in our souls, constrained us to prevent an injustice.

"Has this man committed any sin? No. Has he voluntarily carried out any action that might be prejudicial to us? No. Far from it—he is unfortunate, he has suffered—and the instinct of good will that is within us dictates that we be generous and hospitable toward him. Thus, I have told him that he is free. We have no more right to strike him than to constrain him to remain among us."

"The security of the republic is the supreme law."

"Evil and injustice have never saved a cause, but have always doomed it. In my turn, I appeal to the children here present, who are not conservers of the past but the workers of the future; I ask them this question: Is this man here present guilty?"

And every voice cried, at the same time: "No! No! A thousand times no!"

"Then you do not accept that he should be punished…?"

"Punished? For what? Why? It's unjust. We cannot accept it!"

"Ancestors, inheritors of the rancor and wrath of our ancestors, you have heard what your children say. Humankind once treated us badly, but the people of today are not responsible for their forefathers' misdeeds. We set aside and annul the sentence passed by the High Court. Stranger, we hold our hands out to you honestly. If you wish, you shall be one of us, in full security and full equality."

I had advanced toward the young president and offered him both my hands; applause rang out.

In vain, the old men of the High Court protested, crying that all was lost, that the foundations of society had been broken, and that its collapse would be frightful.

The young president—my savior—who was named Jean Lefèvre, had draw me out of the courtroom on to the exterior terrace, where the schoolchildren awaiting the result of the deliberation uttered cries of joy when they saw me. Never, I must admit, had my appearance provoked such enthusiasm—to the extent that I could not help a certain sensation of vanity, and I waved my hand politely, like a sovereign in the midst of my subjects. Then, still guided by my savior, I arrived at the edge of the balcony overlooking the city.

At that moment, an exceedingly lively fanfare burst forth, formed of notes grouped in a singular rhythm.

Doctor Durand came over to me. "You don't understand?" he said.

"What are you talking about?"

"Those sounds that you hear—which are a language. Listen—don't you perceive that: ta... tat a ta... tata... ta... ta, ta, tata!"

"Yes, indeed," I replied.

"Well, that's a phonetic alphabet. The fall of the High Court is being announced to the entire city."

"But that's the principle of the Morse alphabet!" I exclaimed.

"I don't know what you're referring to....but listen to the modulations, the grouping of the notes of the scale in countless combinations. It's an entire language."

I remembered then a musical vocabulary invented in our own land by Sudre.[11] We had not made any use of it.

---

[11] The musician Jean-François Sudre (1787-1862) published his *Langue musicale universelle* in 1862 to promote Solresol, a language with only seven syllables, which could be

At that moment, I saw the young woman who had been charged with phonothanatizing me passing close by. Hiding her cithara in the folds of her white dress, she was slipping through the crowd, seemingly avoiding me. Did she think, then, that I harbored a grudge against her for the mission that she had been constrained to fulfill? Still retaining in my ears the charm of her strange and melodic music, however, I could not forget the auditory delights that I owed to her.

I said as much to Doctor Durand, who smiled. "You're right," he murmured, "not to impute any responsibility for the cruel act to that child, for she's the one who saved you."

"What do you mean?"

"I know from a reliable source that she was fully informed of the plot hatched by the young people. I was surprised myself that the effects of the murderous Phonia were so slow. She prolonged the harmony to give your saviors the time to intervene."

I was so glad of this revelation—for it would have been painful for me to hate the young woman—that I ran to her. "Oh, thank you!" I cried. "I know now that I owe you my life. You are an angel!"

Surprised by my urgency, she recoiled slightly; perhaps she had dreaded some violent word or reproach on my part—but my attitude reassured her rapidly. She gave me a delightful smile—a smile that was infinitely sweet for me—and took the hand that I held out to her.

"You're from Paris then?" she asked. "The other one—the real one?"

"Yes, Mademoiselle."

---

represented by musical notes or colors. It gave rise to a brief fad but never caught on.

"Do the French still dress well?"

"Better and better," I said, laughing. I can assure you that fashions have made great progress—and, charming as your costume is, I can tell you that our fabrics are softer and more flexible than yours."

"Really? And yet, my dress"—she pointed to the white peplum that enveloped her—"is made of the lightest asbestos fabric that we can make..."

A stir in the crowd interrupted the conversation. Doctor Durand came to fetch me and led me to a vultural basket that awaited me, where he took his place along with the young president, the amiable Jean Lefèvre.

With a boldness of which I would not have thought myself capable, however, I took the liberty of summoning my young executioner—whose name, I soon learned, was Isabelle Duval—and, the bird having extended its wings, we descended to the city.

Thus far, the vicissitudes that I endured and the dangers I ran have prevented me from giving the reader of this manuscript a precise idea of that singular locality, a French flower blooming in the wake of astonishing cataclysms in the middle of the Gobi desert.

Some people affirm that that vast expanse of desolation was formed in the wake of a prehistoric catastrophe analogous to the sinking of Atlantis or the engulfing of Lemuria. I have no intention of involving myself in such obscure questions. All I know is that the desert is virtually unknown, that the intemperance of the seasons there is so harsh that caravans rarely attempt to cross it, and then only in the direction of Irkutsk—which is to say, the part closest to Chinese territory.

The oasis of stone that constitutes the mysterious city must be almost in the middle of the desert, in the direction of Tibet. The basalt wall that surrounds it and offers no apparent exit, has a minimum height of 160 meters and a maximum of 500 or 600, which is to say that it is absolutely insurmountable, unless one brings to the foot of those enormous masses—whose smooth surfaces prevent their being scaled—mechanical engines of exceptional power and complexity.

On the other hand, though, you will understand that that circular surround protects its inhabitants against the dry wind that blows from Siberia and the glacial sea. Who would have guessed, or imagined, behind those black ramparts, where all life seemed to stop, the existence of a group of human beings, more isolated from the world than if they had been exiled to a Pacific island?

Now, these people, these Frenchmen, mostly Parisian in origin, had been separated from the rest of humankind during the earliest years of the 18th century—between 1703 and 1705, most probably—and since then had been cut off from the scientific and industrial advancement that had shaped our society. When Fate imprisoned them in that yoke of rocks, the most learned among them were ignorant of the basic elements of modern knowledge. The soil on which they ran aground was unproductive; all the ordinary resources of life were lacking. The basaltic rock formed the foundations, the terrain and the perimeter of their habitat alike. There was no earth, no water, no animals and no vegetation; imagine an immense crater in which the lava is frozen, a black, slick basin in which it is scarcely possible to keep one's footing! What horror those unfortunates must have felt! How is it that those sequestered men and women did not succumb to despair and terror?

Well, they survived.

Now that I have taken my place among them and have become acclimatized to this unsuspected Paris, I cannot find expressions that paint with sufficient force that admiration experienced by the civilized man that I am before the energy, tenacity and ingenuity of what these people have accomplished.

As you shall see, staring from the same point as us, when the positive, mechanical, chemical and physical sciences were still in a rudimentary state, they have headed in a different direction from the one we have followed, in terms of both material life and social organization. Was their orientation better or worse than ours? That is for others to decide. I shall relate what I know, what I have seen and what I appreciate, without making any comparisons between my erstwhile compatriots and my present ones.

According to the latest census, the inhabitants of Paris number 2885; the small number of the initial inhabitants and the difficulties of life are sufficient explanation of the smallness of this number.

The first problem that faced them was elementary: they had to eat.

I have already mentioned the struggle that they had to undertake against monstrous birds; for long years they were their only prey. A few grassy plants, lichens, mosses and saxifrages plucked from fissures in the rocks, disgusting reptiles they had to destroy in order not to perish in their poisonous embraces—such were the efforts of nature in favor of those wretches. Let us see what followed.

You will remember that since my arrival in the territory I had only had one meal—and what a meal! To be sure, I do not deny that the fluid that emerged from the strangely-formed flasks tasted exquisite, and that the bizarre provender in question had given me the illusion of sustenance...but it has been a long time since philosophers first remarked that illusion is not very nutritious—and, in fact, my appetite had returned with a surprising rapidity. Perhaps the preparations of the Phonothanatos had hastened my digestion.

At any rate, while I went down to the city in the vulture-car with my three friends, the doctor, the young president and my amiable musical executioner, I felt such sharp hunger pangs that I could not help putting my hand to my stomach and exclaiming, Oh, how hungry I am!"

"I understand," said Doctor Durand. "Your organs have not yet adapted to our analytical nourishment. I was I such haste to sustain you, in order to give you the strength to resist the anguish that awaited you, that I served you whatever I had ready to hand—which is to say, chemical conserves formed of the constituent elements of foodstuffs, with the appropriate tastes and nutritional qualities."[12]

"But that's Berthelot's cuisine!" I exclaimed.

---

[12] Lermina inserts a footnote here: "Author's note: It is well-known that a human being, for his daily refection, needs to absorb 21 grams of nitrogen and 310 grams of carbon." Lermina had written other stories employing the motif of the chemical synthesis of foodstuffs from their constituent elements—see, for instance, "Quiet House" in the Black Coat Press anthology *The Germans on Venus*, a volume that also includes Charles Nodier's "Perfectibility," in which the Patagons nourish themselves in a similar manner. The notion was popularized in France by Marcellin Berthelot (1827-1907), who synthesized numerous hydrocarbons and anticipated a glorious future for such techniques in *Chimie organique fondée sur la synthèse* (1860).

"Who's Berthelot?"

"Our greatest chemist. He predicted that within a century we would be nourishing ourselves on carbon, hydrogen and oxygen, with a pinch of nitrogen to season it all."

"I don't understand any of the words you've just pronounced," said Jean Lefèvre, "but I deduce that you're talking about the elementary gases of substance. Carbon must be our carbonal fluid, hydrogen our aqual fluid, oxygen the rubigal."

"Indeed," I interrupted, "those Latin-rooted words have the same meanings as our chemical terms borrowed from the Greek: oxy means rust, like rubigo, aqua is water, like hydro…"

"Quite so. Still, it's more than 150 years since our forefathers tried to reconstitute, in accordance with the gustatory memories of the oldest among them, the foodstuffs with which they had formerly been familiar in their own country."

"But we have better ones than those nowadays," said young Isabelle, "And if you'll permit it, I'll give you certain synthetic foodstuffs to taste…"

The conversation was interrupted by a slight shock. We had just landed.

I had been so preoccupied with that chemico-culinary discussion that I had not noticed the rapidity of our descent, and I suddenly found myself in a grand plaza filled with a crowd that, on seeing me, cheered me yet again.

I was definitely a celebrity.

It seemed, moreover, that the entire population of the country was keenly interested in my fate, and had encouraged the schoolchildren in the revolutionary expedition that they had just completed. A few voices even shouted: "Down with the High Court!"—and I firmly believe that if the old judges had been there, they would have endured an exceedingly uncomfortable quarter of an hour.

Personally, I was momentarily fearful of being the object of an overly violent enthusiasm. A hundred hands were extended to shake mine; the women, especially, seemed desirous of palpating my clothing. Perhaps they saw me as a magician, contact with whom might be actively favorable, or perhaps here, as elsewhere, matters of fashion and costume took the foremost rank in feminine preoccupations.

Meanwhile, I looked around. I was not a little surprised to see the Hôtel de Ville on one side of the plaza where the crowd were pressing. Yes—our Hôtel de Ville! Not, it is true, the one that I had left behind me on my last passage through Paris, but one very similar to the one I remembered seeing many times over in engraving in illustrated magazines, and even in Germain Brice's "Description of Paris,"[13] with its campanile, its two wings, the equestrian statue of Henri IV in bas-relief above the main door, and the sets of pillars forming galleries. And I understood that I had before my eyes an exact reproduction of the Hôtel de Ville as it had been under Louis XIV.

I expressed my astonishment to Jean Lefèvre, who replied: "Why the excitement? Isn't it only natural that our forefathers attempted to reconstitute, in their distant Paris, the marvelous memories of the great city that they

---

[13] *Description nouvelle de ce qu'il y a de plus remarquable dans la ville de Paris* by Germain Brice, first published in 1685 and reprinted nine times, was the first "tourist guide" to the city.

had brought with them? They loved their homeland and, although they were resigned to be separated from it forever, they conserved nevertheless a slight regret for the past. And who will tell you that we ourselves don't sometimes experience a strange and vague desire…?" He stopped, and passed his hand over his forehead as if to expel an importunate thought. "In brief," he went on, "you'll find all the names of ancient France here, of Paris particularly, insofar as they are featured on a plan that one of our people once reconstituted from memory, after that of a certain Gomboust[14]…in a little while, I'll take you to the Louvre."

"Bah!" I cried. "The Louvre! Have you a king to accommodate, then?"[15]

"Certainly not—and yet, it's one of our most important edifices. You'll doubtless be of the same opinion when you know that the Louvre is our national Refectory."

At that moment, the sound of trumpets rang out. Immediately, I saw the crowd separate into groups and then form lines in the manner of children coming out of school. They started marching in the same direction.

Jean had steered me toward one of these groups, which was made up of men with intelligent and serious faces. As if they had been alerted to the strangeness of my arrival among them, they all looked at me with interest, certainly without any malevolence, and trying hard

---

[14] Jacques Gomboust, Louis XIV's *ingénieur du roi*, was the first person to apply the principles of geometry to the mapping of Paris, producing his first such plan in 1647 and a more comprehensive one, which was widely reproduced, in 1652.
[15] The Louvre was, of course, a royal palace before it was converted into a museum.

not to trouble me with manifestations of indiscreet curiosity.

We went along a street that bore the exceedingly singular name of Vallée-de-Misère—which, Jean explained, had been given in the 17th century to the quai that led from the Hôtel de Ville to the Louvre. These good people were definitely much better informed than I was as to the topography of Old Paris.

"Do you have a watercourse in your Paris?" asked Jean, while walking beside me.

"It's called a river—one of the finest in France, the Seine."

"We have no rivers or watercourses," said my interlocutor, with a hint of sadness in his voice, "but we have our Seine."

"Really? But you said you had no rivers."

"We have given that name, which sounds so sweetly in the ear, to a long and broad esplanade, which separates our city into two parts. Look."

I followed the indication of his gesture and I saw a sort of long garden which extended through the entire extent of the city, from one basalt wall to the other. It contained a sort of fleece of arborescent plants.

"You have cultivation, then?"

"A hundred years ago, our fathers began carefully to collect the soil that the wind brought us, and which the rain removed and washed down from fissures in the rock. At about the same time, we had almost succeeded in fabricating it..."

"Fabricating soil?"

"Why not? Isn't it formed of mineral elements, like everything else that exists? Little by little, they were able to constitute a layer—of very moderate thickness, it's true, but which certainly contains the seeds of numerous vegetable products. While awaiting their useful development, we installed therein the grassy plants, lichens and climbing plants that grow spontaneously in our caves or upon our wall; we have cared for them, directed and modified them, and gradually assembled this flora—which, you will agree, is pleasant in appearance."

The fact is that I was dazzled by the bright coloration of some of the flowers, some of which were vivid red or fiery yellow, with brown or white strips—veritable curiosities that could scarcely have been matched by the newest varieties of our old world.

"You're looking at the shades," Jean Lefèvre said. "They seem slightly baroque to you. I should tell you that they're only experiments in coloration obtained by hyporacinic injections."

"What does that mean?"

"That we've attempted to infuse various mineral essences into the roots—copper, iron and so on—in carefully measured doses. We're obtaining the strangest esthetic effects, but we're persevering and we're succeeding in reconstituting the brightest hues as well as the softest..." He interrupted himself. "We've arrived," he said. "I expect that little stroll has given you an appetite."

Indeed, the view of that Seine with florescent waves had, so to speak, aggravated my stomach. I went into the Louvre.

To be honest, the building that had been decorated with that historic name bore little resemblance to the sumptuous monument of stone that sheltered the glory of our kings for such a long time. As on the bank of our river, however, there was a long gallery that extended over a space I estimated to be 200 square meters. It must have been 10 or 12 meters in height. It was like a scale model of the Hall of Machines, except that its framework, instead of being made of iron, was made up of stone colonnettes, resembling onyx, jade and porphyry, fully garnished with immense windows.

Numerous doors gave access to the interior. Above the main entrance there was a bust, almost colossal in its dimensions, slightly primitive in execution, but with a truly extraordinary intensity of expression. I read on a placard the name LEBRUN XXVI. Who was this hero? I was later to discover that he was the inventor of *analytical cuisine*. At the time, I did not have the opportunity to enquire. My young friend had drawn me gently to one of the doors.

I went in, and an exclamation of sincere admiration escaped my lips. The room into which I had been introduced was marvelous in its grandeur, its proportions, its lighting, its beauty and, I must say, its dazzling luxury. Never, in our most luxurious palaces or our most opulent châteaux, had I contemplated a gallery more harmonious in its construction, ornamented more tastefully, giving a more intense sensation of wealth and comfort or—what made the deepest impression on me—painted in more delicately harmonized colors. That room welcomed you with a smile.

Then there was the floral decoration deployed on all sides, which made me open my eyes wide. There were enormous bouquets of...what flowers were they? They were vaguely reminiscent of dahlias, of carnations, of wisterias, of jasmines, of lilies...and yet not quite the same. The tulips were admirable, the sunflowers resplendent, the lilac-blossom delicate and elegant. But in all these flowers, which sprang forth like rockets and fell back in clusters, interlacing in sheaves, I could not recognize exactly those of my homeland. Their sizes and shapes were not analogous, their forms were more regular and—how can I put it?—more mathematical.

A sweet joy was in store for me; at the first step I took into the room, Isabelle, very gracious and blushing slightly, overtook me and presented me with a rose, a masterpiece of design and color—and when I lifted it to my face, thanking the charming donor with a tender gaze, I perceived an exquisite odor, the quintessence of the emanation of roses.

My guide summoned me. I went on.

He had definitely told me that this was a refectory, but to tell the truth, it bore no resemblance whatsoever, in terms of its fittings, to those with which we are familiar, and describe as fashionable restaurants. It was, instead, an immense hall formed by an infinity of small rooms separated from one another by hedges of greenery and flowers—which, I soon discovered, were mobile, and could be assembled into booths of various sizes at the whim of the guests.

These *salonnets*—simultaneously isolated from and juxtaposed with others—were furnished with comfortable seats grouped in pairs, fours or sixes, or even greater numbers, in such a way as to permit any number of guests to form particular companies. In front of each chair was a little table, on which I observed a variety of apparatus—phials and rounded flasks—similar to those which had already been presented to me during the last meal to which I had been invited. In front of these flasks was a sort of keyboard, like that of a typewriter, which was connected to the flasks by little tubes. Each of the guests was equipped with an amber tip, which he lifted to his lips in his left hand, while the other lightly pressed the keys.

The amber tip was, of course, personal, and I saw that everyone carried one on his person, carefully enclosed in a case.

Our company was composed of mature men and a few women; it was like a little bourgeois family. I was placed between Doctor Durand and my young friend Jean Lefèvre, for whom I experienced an incessantly increasing sympathy.

"Well," said the doctor, "I expect this meal will please you more than its predecessor—but I must now initiate you into the mysteries of our culinary art. Examine each of these flasks; they bear engraved labels. The symbols on these labels are incomprehensible to you, but to us they signify the nutritive and gustatory element that is to be found in each flask."

At this point, he gave me a list—in terms unintelligible to me, the scientific terminology of the country being entirely different from ours. In common parlance, however, he meant that each of the flasks contained combinations of nitrogen, carbon, oxygen and so on, whose juxtaposition, obtained by manipulating the keys, gave the sensation of the most exquisite foodstuffs, at the same time as the chemical elements played their nutritive role of reconstitution.

"The science of eating," Doctor Durand explained, "is constituted by the delicacy of the fingering, and the choice of harmonious combinations. Come on, set yourself in front of the keyboard. Here's a new amber mouthpiece."

So saying, Durand placed in front of me a sheet of simili-cardboard, on which cabalistic signs were inscribed, which were reproduced on the keys. In sum, it was an eating machine entirely analogous to our typewriters. The symbols on the card were equivalent to musical notes, with bars, crotchets, quavers, grace notes, etc. On his keyboard, the guest played the culinary piece, whose combinations brought him the requisite tastes, in the same way that we Europeans play a song by Schumann or a sonata by Mozart on the piano. Later, I appreciated the merits of these culinary combinations; just as Beethoven wrote his immortal masterpieces with the seven notes of the scale, so culinary composers wrote alimentary symphonies with the 18 nutritive and gustatory elements whose scale was established here, which realized the ideals of the most delicate gourmets.

These harmonies had first been created by those ancestors who had lived long enough to direct the initial progress of the colony, and it was thanks to them that it had been possible to conserve and reconstitute memories of French cuisine. The last author of the most recherché melodies had died, almost a centenarian, in 1780.

"But of what are these flavors composed?" I asked

"Of mineral combinations," the doctor replied. "I've told you that the first and most difficult problem facing our ancestors was that of alimentation. They had no livestock, and no vegetables—only a few birds, whose meat was tough, and a few fish that arrived—no one knows how—to populate a little lake born of a new and brief convulsion of the ground. It was certain that these resources would be rapidly exhausted. In the short term, they faced death by starvation: the slowest and most horrible of all.

"It was then that an alchemist—one of those savants who had once been pursued and burned—on studying the minerals that formed the wall of our prison, made the astonishing discovery of nutritive elements contained in so-called inorganic matter, separated the gases, analyzed the salts and created metallophagy from scratch! You're looking at the tables compiled by Lebrun 26, our true savior—but progress is difficult and prejudice is resistant! It required an incredible struggle to persuade people who were literally dying of starvation to accept scientific alimentation.

"In your civilization, I'm sure, you must have undertaken numerous battles against established routine, but none, I can assure you, can have attained the violence of ours. Women, especially, revealed themselves to be furiously intransigent; they wanted to nourish themselves entirely on vulture preserves, and perished. In 1789, there was an explosion; a dictatorial government was established and—I'm ashamed to say—the national alembic was set up in the public square, to which the recalcitrant were dragged, and subjected to scientific force-feeding.

"Furthermore, there were sometimes accidents, as in any period of experimentation. Some people were overdosed with phosphoric acid, some with nitrogen, some with synthetic fats, which resulted in indigestion. Our scientists were organized into a Committee for Public Safety; some of them proved pitiless, and there were regrettable plethoras.

"Sad memories—but how glorious, when we think that, without those victims and martyrs, life would have been long extinct within this ring of stone. On the contrary, since that year 89, chemical alimentation has developed in conditions of incessant amelioration. You are now in the national refectory, where the entire population gathers at certain times, and you can see that it is healthy and vigorous."

While he was speaking I had tried to position my fingers on the keyboard, selecting notes identical to those represented on the cardboard—on the score, if you wish. I was still maladroit, however; the flavors flooded my mouth, devoid of rhythm, with over-emphatic contrasts. The indefatigable Jean Lefèvre came to the rescue, and I was impressed by his virtuosity.

What a marvel! Beneath his agile fingers, the flavors flowed, forming thirds, fifths and octaves. There was one diminished seventh that carried me away. What tender trills! What flourishes of exquisite papillae!

I was astounded; I had great difficulty in hitting the right pitch. Ws it really possible that human beings, deprived of all the alimentary resources with which we are familiar—poultry, livestock, fish, game, eggs, vegetables and fruits—had solved a problem only recently sketched out by our great chemist Berthelot?

On looking around, I observed a number of details that amazed me. It was the entire population, nearly three thousand human beings, that had gathered in the Great National Refectory. Imagine a banquet of that size among us! What a racket of crockery, silverware and crystal! Imagine those three thousand jaws chewing heartily at the same time, six thousand arms performing contortions over three thousand plates, their gestures armed with forks and knives—and all arranged in long lines, with a place for each one so restricted that everyone's knees were bumping into one another and their elbows jammed up against one another.

Here, everything is spacious and comfortable. Three or four hundred groups are installed, as if in little nooks of greenery, on comfortable seats, having little machines at their disposal that are elegant in form and do not take up too much space. The fingers are agile, the ladies gracious in their gestures. And, while sucking at the amber mouthpieces, people chat.

Since then, I have learned and appreciated the fact that chemical nourishment is so easily digested that the stomach seems to have become unnecessary—to the extent that, in accordance with the theories of our Metchnikoff,[16] there is talk of the possible ablation of that inconvenient organ.

That immense refectory—whose luxury, as I have said, was truly admirable—bore some resemblance to an upper-class casino, to a club in the best possible taste, where ideas were exchanged in the most placid leisure.

Jean whispered in my ear: "What would you say to a romance in pineapple?"

I consented.

Very delicately, with a supreme lightness of hand, my young friend picked out the advertised dish on my keyboard. It was delicious! I confess, however, that—perhaps by auto-suggestion—it seemed to me that that fluidic nourishment was not sufficiently filling.

It was then that young Isabelle appeared at the back of the room, carrying a golden dish, like an ancient choëphorus.[17] She was walking slowly, almost like a priestess. A ripple of curiosity ran around the room. For the first time since the beginning of the meal, there was a

---

[16] "Our Metchnikoff" was actually the Russian Ilya Metchnikov (1845-1916), although the French re-christened him "Elie" when he arrived in Paris to work for the Pasteur Institute in 1888. He was best known for his work on the immune system, and it is in that context that he used the word "ablation" (wasting away); the notion that unused organs would atrophy and gradually disappear was actually much older.

[17] A Greek term most familiar nowadays by virtue of its plural use in the title of the second part of Aeshylus' *Oresteia*, usually translated as *The Libation-Bearers*.

stir. Ranks were formed; people jostled to get a better view.

Jean leaned toward me and said, merrily: "Another revolution, perhaps!"

A small table had been hurriedly set before me, with a tablecloth—then a plate and a knife.

The choëphorus was still drawing nearer. Exclamations mingled with questions. "Oh, that's pretty! That must be good!" And young Isabelle, still exquisite and still blushing slightly, set the golden dish in front of me and said, simply: "Natural lamb cutlet!"

Suddenly, there was a solemn, almost religious, silence. I discovered the reason later.

In the vulture-car, Isabelle had spoken mysteriously about certain foodstuffs whose nature she had not explained. It was a matter of a turning point in the culinary history of the young republic. A scientist, endowed with a boldness that had caused his theories to attract the epithet "heretical", had taken it into his head to reconstitute not only the elements of alimentation but even the very form and substance of various foodstuffs, and restore their material tangibility. The result of his research and his arduous labors was in front of me: a synthetic cutlet!

Its appearance was, in fact, perfect; it really was a cutlet, with a succulent nucleus, golden-brown in color, with a modest and appetizing strip of fat along the bone.

At that evocation of the absent fatherland, I felt tears forming in the corners of my eyes.

All eyes were fixed upon me. Children had climbed up the colonnettes in order to bombard me with their plunging gazes.

Isabelle, delighted to be bringing me this early fruit of a great discovery, was gradually moving backwards, crossing her hands over her breast in a virginal gesture.

My dining-companions were standing up. Doctor Durand was a trifle pale.

I took up the knife, then, and I attacked…

Beating hearts were audible.

Oh, what strength of character, what an energetic impassivity I required!

It was spongy, flaccid, insipid and pasty—atrocious! And yet, the difficult problem had been solved of evoking, beneath all of that, the taste of burnt rancid fat!

Stoically, I swallowed…and I smiled.

There was thunderous applause.

Then, desirous of proving my courtesy, my disinterest and my absolute absence of egotism, I got up abruptly and politely forced Doctor Durand to take my place. I presented him with a morsel of the thing on the end of my knife.

His palate enticed, he took it in his lips and into his mouth, and chewed.

He looked at me. I looked at him. That meant that we were looking at one another.

The public applauded wholeheartedly.

"Excellent!" said the doctor.

"Exquisite!" I replied.

Then the doctor, leaning close to my ear, whispered: "Genius has its errors!"

That cutlet was indeed a work of genius: a marvelous composition of anthracite, barytes and strontia, which reeked of old burnt candle-wax!

VIII.

I don't know whether or not my inexperience in organizing the digestion of chemico-organic cuisine was the cause of the sudden weariness that oppressed me at the end of that meal. Perhaps it was simply explicable by the fatigue of the previous days and the emotions that had over-excited my nervous system. At any rate, I confided to my excellent friend Durand that I had an overwhelming need for rest, and that my greatest desire was to lie down and go to sleep.

"That won't do," the fine fellow said. "We'll get you fixed up as best we can." Then, turning to Jean, who was ever-ready to be of service, he said: "Which room can we use?"

"Number 127 has just become free; its tenant has got married and taken 250. It's quite close to me—it will be very easy for me to keep an eye on our cherished guest."

"That's perfect—except that you live some distance away, and I don't think our friend is in any state to walk far."

That's my opinion too," said Jean, "but we have the aromal claw, haven't we?"

"Claw!" I exclaimed, not without a certain anxiety. "Aromal!" I was not yet experienced in the vocabulary of these good people, and was in constant fear of some new eccentricity.

"Now, now—don't be afraid!" said my young friend, laughing. "We understand from the exclamations you utter that everything here seems bizarre to you. What do you expect? Your civilization, of which we

113

know nothing, could not have ended up in the same place, although it had the same departure point. We shall doubtless have an opportunity, someday soon, to investigate that question thoroughly; from now on, just accept that we haven't followed the same path. For the moment, take advantage of our inventions as we would have made use of yours, on the simple affirmation that that they have been tried and tested, and believe in their utility. You wouldn't hesitate, would you, if one of us were to stray into the Paris of which you are so proud, to entrust him to your machines?"

"Of course! And it will be a veritable pleasure for me to teach you about the employment of steam, electricity, railways, telegraphy, the telephone, the Metropolitain…oh, the Metropolitain!"

"All words that sound barbaric to our ears, and which—I will take your word for it—conceal marvels. In the same way, have faith in us, give us credit until everything has been demonstrated—and don't disdain the aromal claw in advance."

I stifled a yawn. "As you wish! I hand myself over to you, bound hand and foot, come what may!"

My words certainly did not give evidence of an absolute confidence, but my new friends did not seem to take offense.

It was not easy to get out of that crowd, whose members, avid to study me, pressed around me as I went. Finally, thanks to me companions, I was able to escape those slightly excessive expressions of sympathy, and we found ourselves some distance away from the Louvre.

"The Place du Palais-Royal," Jean Lefèvre informed me.

I replied with a gesture of indifference; although the name was the same, it has to be admitted that the resemblance between our Place du Palais-Royal and that one was far from perfect. This one was surrounded on three sides by vast buildings, whose architecture was almost identical to that of the Louvre.

"These are our public schools," said Jean. "It was from here that we departed to snatch you from the execution-chamber."

"Many thanks! You arrived just in time. Hold on—the Obelisk!" That exclamation had been provoked by the sight of an exceedingly tall pylon of some that reminded me of the needle of Luxor. Its tip was higher than all the surrounding buildings. In addition to the fact that it was not decorated with any hieroglyphs, it differed from our Obelisk—about which the people of the seventeenth century could not have known, since it was erected under Louis-Philippe[18]—in that its upper section bore an immense horizontal arm, like a colossal lever, which extended as far as the eye could see, silhouetted against the sky.

Jean whistled softly. A man emerged from a little building nearby, pushing a kind of box in front of him, which was somewhat reminiscent of our ancient Sedan chairs. The man went to the pylon and pressed a switch. A chain unrolled from above.

I did not understand; in spite of the effort I made to conserve my self-composure, I could not help seeming anxious.

"Don't worry," said Jean. "I'll go with you. Don't be afraid."

---

[18] In 1835, to be precise, in the Place de la Concorde.

"Afraid?" I said, straightening up. "I've seen many others."

The box had been positioned under the chain; at the extremity of the chain there was a claw, which had just engaged with a ring fixed on top of the Sedan chair.

Jean opened the door of the box. "Get in," he said. Then, addressing the young man, who seemed to be awaiting orders like a respectful coachman—a coachman with neither carriage nor horses—he said: "To 127-5-33!"

I was comfortably seated, with a slight chill in my back. There was a grating sound. The chain stretched, and lifted up the box, with us inside it. I clung on to my seat.

We climbed rapidly up into the air; through the window of the box I perceived that we had arrived at the height of the lever, which bore inscriptions and numbers. We slid along the arm, and I observed that we stopped at notch 127. We had passed over a part of the city. The lever began to rotate above the houses, like the arm of one of the cranes we use to unload sacks of apples or other commodities; then it stopped abruptly. I felt a slight nausea. Suddenly, the chain unrolled, and we descended so rapidly that it seemed to me that, this time, we were going to smash into the ground. "Stop!" I yelled, at the top of my voice.

"Not before you're home," said Jean, sniggering.

We reached the roof of a building; evidently, our vehicle was about to crash and we would be thrown to the ground, in a pitiful state.

Not at all. The roof opened to let us pass through. And the chair stopped, settling with a slight shock.

"Here we are, in residence," said my young friend, opening the door and offering me his arm, like a great lord to a lady at Versailles. I got out, without knowing exactly what I was doing.

I found myself in a brightly-lit and very spacious room, in which, to my great joy, my first glance fell upon a bed. Oh, to sleep! The rest of the furniture was of scant importance to me.

The portable chair climbed up again and disappeared silently through a bay in the ceiling, which closed again automatically. We were alone.

"That's marvelous!" I exclaimed, more out of politeness than conviction.

"Yes," said the young man, negligently. "A new invention that has not yet reached its full development. It's the first application of a recently-discovered motive force, from which we expect great results—but I mustn't abuse your patience any longer. Here you are, at home, lord and master of this room and its annexes. You doubtless need to refresh your body by means of a few ablutions...."

"I dared not ask...a shower would be very welcome."

"Good," said Jean, opening a little door. "Go in here..."

I took a step forward, then recoiled. "What, into that black room?"

"Once again, have a little trust. Go in and get undressed. I'll serve as a bath-attendant for you..."

"Explain to me, I beg you, what is about to happen."

"You're going to take a photic shower, and you'll tell me what you think of it..."

He helped me to undress. My eyes adapted to the darkness, and I saw a sort of tub, above which was an apparatus almost exactly similar to our showers, composed of tubes.

"Very god!" said Jean. "I'll start it..."

He pulled a cord, and from the tubes in question emerged jets....of white light, with a slight pink tint, which—I can't think of any other way to put it—sprinkled me from my feet to my head. Then light rained down upon my head, spring forth from all sides; I was enveloped in a network of colored jets, which intersected one another and mingled together, brushing me and touching me all over. The sensation was exquisite, simultaneously gentle and penetrating.

"The photic shower," Jen aid to me, "from the Latin *phos*, light, has had to replace aqueous ablutions among us, but it rids the body of all impurities better than water, and in addition, imparts relief and comfort, as you can observe."

"That's true! Oh, all this is quite astonishing."

"Good! Now go to bed and sleep..."

"Oh, my God, what a pity! Stay with me for a few minutes more and give me a few explanations. There's one thing haunting me. What, then, are your motive forces?"

"As we don't have at our disposal either waterfalls or air-currents, we've been obliged to utilize the forces that nature does put at our disposal—which is to say, sound, light and perfume."

"What! Sound! Perfume! I don't understand a single word of what you've just said."

"You surprise me greatly, in my turn," the young man replied. "You don't utilize the incalculable power of sound?"

"For organs and trumpets, nothing more."

"What about light?"

"We illuminate our surroundings with…"

"Which is to say that you don't transform it—you don't make a docile slave of it. What about perfume?"

"We condense it in little bottles, and diffuse it over our underclothing by means of droplet-sprays."

"And then? Nothing more? You don't know anything about channeled sound, compressed perfume?"

The joke seemed to me to have gone beyond acceptable limits. "I beg your pardon," I said to my complacent conversationalist, "but in truth I think my brain is a little too weary to take aboard these ideas—which are, to say the least, bizarre. It would be better, I think, if I were to seek in reparative sleep for the strength to understand you…"

"So be it," said Jean, seemingly slightly piqued. "Only remember the single phrase that is the quintessence of science, and which was produced no less than a hundred and fifty years ago by our great Mathieu Dupont 24: *Nothing exists but vibrations!*"

"That's quite possible," I said, yawning mightily.

And I fell asleep on the spot.

IX.

It might become overly complicated if I were to record all the stages through which I was obliged to pass in order to be initiated into the knowledge of these astonishing people, who, starting from the most absolute deprivation, left without resources and without scientific sophistication—the baggage that a 17th century savant lugged around is well-known—by virtue to their tenacity and their energy, had achieved great practical progress and realized the most powerful inventions.

Sound! Perfume! Light! For us, these manifestations of natural force have remained at the level of facts observed but not utilized, while here, they form the basis of mechanical science, and by means of which machines are animated, compared with which our most powerful engines seem almost to be childish playthings.

But enough of reflections—I shall get on with my story.

In the morning, I woke up to sunlight transmitted through the colored windows in my ceiling. I had never felt more refreshed or healthier. I was able to examine my bedroom at my leisure.

To tell the truth, there was nothing very unusual about it, except that it was very bright and spacious. I found out subsequently that all the houses similarly consisted of a simple ground floor lit from above—which is explicable by the configuration of the locality, over which high walls of rock projected their eternal shadow.

For the first time, I looked quite carefully at the objects surrounding me: the bed, the chairs and a table. First, I observed that not one of these items of furniture had any angular projection. Everything was rounded, as if to spare the inhabitant any disagreeable bumps-and I recalled a certain Parisian bed adorned with a certain night-stand, which jabbed my legs or my sides with the ridges of their ornamentation every time I got up.

The bedclothes in which I had curled up attracted my attention. I tried to identify the fabric, and I suddenly realized that, lacking linen and cloth, they had invented mineral textiles unknown to me. I found out later that they had, in fact, employed an ingenious application of pulverized stone in the manufacture of the fabrics currently in use.

The sheets were made from a mineral paste broadly analogous to that of our paper, in which the feathers of birds formed the resistant weft. It was the same for other fabrics, including those in clothing. They had also succeeded in laminating metals and reducing them to such a thinness that they became pliable, adaptable to all kinds of uses; to facilitate their movements, they had articulations built into them, systems of lamina resembling those of Japanese blinds. Women's clothes, for formal wear, were made of asbestos.

Mica had been utilized for windows; schists, quartzes and slates found their employment in many everyday objects. The colonnettes of houses were made of feldspar; plutonic stones and granites were worked with a finesse testifying to an art full of taste and delicacy.

As soon as I had got up, I had—in accordance with an old habit—taken my light bath. You can see that I was acclimatizing. I found a new suit of clothes at the foot of my bed, whose make-up I was able to study at my leisure. Its form was a trifle outdated; I had a doublet, breeches, and stockings in the style of a clerk at the

Montagne Sainte-Geneviève.[19] These mineralo-metallic fabrics were inconvenienced, in spite of everything, by a certain stiffness; they were rough, but I rapidly became accustomed to them, and felt no more than a slight annoyance.

While I was philosophizing about these curious things, Jean came in. He shook my by the hand politely and enquired as to my health, anxious about the possible consequences of my excitement and fatigue.

"I've never felt better," I assured him.

"That's as well," he said, "for you'll be all the more ready to work."

I turned to him abruptly. "To work?" I said. "What do you mean?"

With the most perfect tranquility, he continued: "I suppose that you're in the habit of eating?"

"Naturally. Every day...rather three times than twice."

"Oh, four times if you like! Then it must seem entirely natural to you to work. Haven't you done so until now?"

"I beg your pardon! I had a private income."

"Ah! Yes, we heard talk of something of that sort at one time. So you remained completely idle?"

"Not at all—but I chose the sort of work I would do. I'm a philologist."

"A very interesting vocation—which, if you remain among us, we would be glad to see you continue. If I'm not mistaken, that kind of work is perfectly agreeable to you..."

---

[19] The Montagne Sainte-Geneviève is a hill on the left bank that was once the site of the Ecole Polytechnique and is still at the heart of the "student quarter" of Paris.

"Absolutely."

"Well, listen to this. Take note, right away, that we don't intend to exercise any kind of constraint upon you. We only operate by persuasion. Everyone here must contribute daily a certain quantity of work: material, effective, let us even say painful—according, of course to his age, his strength and his state of health. In exchange for that he has a right to the satisfaction of his needs; he is entitled to his place at the National Refectory, lodgings, necessary clothing—in a word, everything that is necessary for life.

"It is only when one has furnished one's quota of work that one is a citizen of our Republic, with all the rights stemming from that title. If you intend to remain among us under the title of foreigner, that's all right; our hospitality is granted to you—but would you not feel a thousand times freer if you carried out your duty like everyone else? You would no longer feel obliged to anyone, you would be everyone's equal, and you could occupy yourself with philology entirely at your leisure."

"So," I interjected, with a certain irony, "I must pay for my subsistence—my chemical substance—with ten or 12 hours labor per day…"

"What are you saying? Almost everyone works; the sum of work that has to be done, divided between us, hardly requires four, three, and sometimes even one hour of real labor. And who can complain about it when, that duty being accomplished, one is completely freed from any material care, and, especially, any anxiety for the future? Consider, too, that in these conditions, we are truly free to dispose of our leisure hours as we wish; to devote them to attractive occupations or, if we wish—which is rare—to do nothing at all.

"In this way, every one of our people is an artist, a seeker, a scientist. Everyone, being liberated from the cares of material existence, has a light and active mind; most often, people strive to realize progress which, in profiting everyone, ameliorates the condition of each individual. You've seen the luxury of our National Refectory; each of our public establishments is similar— the schools, the administrative centers and the theaters have attained the maximum possible elegance and comfort.

"At present, we're preoccupied with making our lodgings more sumptuous, and our clothing more perfect. After the hours of labor, everyone—without exception—has but one desire: to improve the environment in which we live. Does all that seem so unreasonable to you? Once more, though, you're our guest, and we won't force you..."

In interrupted him. "I don't intend to enjoy any privilege. I intend to earn my daily bread like everyone else.

"Bread! Oh, if you could teach us to manufacture it..."

"Hmm! Like the cutlets...well, I shall try. For the time being, make what use of me you wish."

We went outside and walked through the streets.

We passed men who were laden down, transporting materials; others, mounted on ladders, were cleaning the lighting apparatus.

"All these laborers," Jean told me, "during their hours of leisure, are writers, poets, actors and would-be-inventors of new devices. Hang on, do you see that fellow sweeping the street so energetically? That's one of our most distinguished painters, and he's sweeping the detritus on to the shovel of a sculptor to whom we gladly attribute genius. Both of them are members of the Academy that we've founded, according to the ideas of Cardinal de Richelieu."

I could not suppress a smile. The vision of Academicians sweeping the Pont des Arts seemed to me to be the last word in comedy.

Imperturbably, Jean continued: "It's necessary to understand that our forefathers, the survivors of the primordial cataclysm, fund themselves confronted by the horrible reality of imminent death, and that they all had to set to work to ensure their daily survival. They were not numerous enough for any parasites to be able to exist at the expense of others, since their combined efforts were scarcely adequate to ensure everyone the necessary provender. Work was, therefore, generally enforced. How could shelters be built if they did not all set their hands to the task? How could the invasion of vultures be resisted if they had not all stuck together, tightly grouped? How could the rocks be attacked if everyone's strength had not been united against the harsh matter?

"Thus from the very first day, the obligation of material labor was forced upon us, both individually and generally. In that era, it was necessary to work twelve, fifteen or twenty hours a day, to restrict one's sleep, to content oneself with detestable nourishment, to lodge in huts, to dress in rags—but in the same way that the effort was communal, it necessarily followed that everyone benefited from the results obtained, and that fact was insensibly transformed into a right.

"They had seen death too close at hand—death by starvation—not to have understood that it is the satisfaction of material, physical needs precedes everything else.

Live first, philosophize later, said an ancient author.[20] Our forefathers were rational enough to follow that logical process, and they convinced themselves, that, whatever social conditions developed subsequently, the obligation of everyone to work would have as its consequence—as its compensation, if you like—the guarantee for everyone of the satisfaction of the elementary needs: nourishment, lodging, clothing.

"As better results were obtained, the time of obligatory work diminished, and today the average is three hours a day. Only one hour is required from the elderly…"

"What! The elderly work?"

"Certainly, unless they are manifestly unable to do so. The surveillance of projects, the verification of accounts. Even children contribute their efforts, in proportion to their development, and thus pay for their education…"

"What about women?"

"And why should they not work? Do they not have their specialties: couture, cuisine, the care and education of children? Like the men, they earn their liberty in this way, the materiality of life being ensured to them…"

"And that pleases them?"

"More than you might think. They are, in consequence, the equals of men, since they have no need of them to live; they have complete moral independence; no question of interest, however slight, intervenes in the gifts they make of their hearts and bodies. Having no concern for the future, they are free of all constraint, and they would not renounce their duty to work—which as-

---

[20] *Primum vivere, deinde philosophari* (Aristotle).

sures them of the exercise of the right to life—for anything in the world."

All this seemed so me to be so far outside the ideas to which I was accustomed that I could find no answer to it. In reality, I found myself profoundly moved.

Jean had not failed to notice the astonishment that had gripped me. "What do you think," he asked, "of the flowers that ornament the Louvre?"

"As it happens, I wanted to ask you where they were cultivated."

"Ha, ha! You were taken in! That's the greatest compliment you could have paid them."

"Why?"

"Because they're made of metal."

"Impossible! I held one in my hand, I breathed in the scent of a rose…"

"Which was offered to you by its author, young Isabelle…"

"Her! But it's a veritable masterpiece! That's her work, then…"

"No, no—that's a hobby. She cuts out, shapes and colors those little marvels in addition to her obligatory work, which she carries out in the laminary service…"

"Laminary?" I replied, in a questioning tone.

"It's analogous to your bleaching. Your linen is a textile, and is recycled. Ours is woven mineral; it's purified by light and then laminated…and the genteel Isabelle is no less a good working girl than a delightful plastic artist, painter and musician. You can see that manual labor has no deleterious effect on mental effort."

"You might be right," I said. "I read a few lines somewhere—yes, it was in one of Renan's books—which come back to memory…" And, striving to remember, I quoted "*Imagine a man, educated and noble in heart, exercising one of those trades that only require a few hours of work; far from the superior life being closed to that man, he would find himself in a position favorable to philosophical development...*[21]

"The man who wrote that is a sage," said Jean. "Here, work is a public service and everyone submits to it gladly, to earn their tranquility and their liberty."

"I didn't much like the refectory..."

"We're quite used to it; nothing is more painful to us than being constrained by some illness to be served at home..."

"What home? Since meals are taken in common, I assume that you also have vast and luxurious dormitories, where everyone lives together and all privacy is impossible..."

"Haven't you just slept at home? Here, every citizen has the right to a private apartment; if two people marry, their lodgings are doubled—tripled and quadrupled when they have children—but they have a home. At meal times, the family goes to the National Refectory where, as you have seen, people organize themselves as they wish. It's the same at the library—for we have our authors and books—the concert-hall and the theater.

"Everyone enjoys the general comforts. We take care to push that as far as possible; we're incessantly ameliorating the conditions of existence and we're all happy, because there isn't a single unfortunate among us. I hope fervently that you'll consent to remain among us, sand I'm certain that you'll adapt easily to our cus-

---

[21] The freethinking historian Ernest Renan (1823-1892) was one of Lermina's heroes. The quotation comes from *L'Avenir de la Science* (1890; tr. as *The Future of Science*).

toms. But here we are at the phonic workshop. There's still time for you to refuse to work. Just say the word and you won't evoke your status s a privileged guest in vain…"

"I don't want to raise any objection—and the experience won't displease me…but I'm damned if I know how I might be useful to you…"

X.

We had crossed the entirety of the city and had arrived at the foot of the highest cliff, an enormous black block more than a hundred meters high.

We went under an immense porch, beyond which a vault was lost to sight in the depths of the mass. From daylight we passed into artificial light produced by globules of mica, in each of which shone something like a star, closely resembling the sparks of our Jablochkoff lamps.[22]

We walked into the midst of a busy crowd of people, coming and going, carrying tools or materials, and arrived in an immense hall in which colossal wheels were rotating with an extraordinary velocity, operating axle-trees that disappeared into lateral galleries.

Men were working there, attentively and interestedly supervising the machines, and I recognized several that I had already seen the day before, at the Louvre or in the plaza in front of the Hôtel de Ville. Now, though, they were dressed in a kind of brown close-fitting protective clothing, doubtless to avoid their being caught up in the terrible engines in hectic motion around them.

Jean played the role of cicerone. Bend over a vast grindstone was the author of a treatise on the origin of worlds; another man, who, it appeared was a historian, was sprinkling talc over the workings of a cylinder. "Our greatest poet," he whispered in my ear, pointing to a

---

[22] Pavel Yablochkov, or Jablochkoff, invented the "Yablochkov candle," an early form of arc lamp, in 1876.

muscular fellow passing by, pushing a trolley in front of him.

Sully-Prudhomme with a wheelbarrow! Rostand with a handcart!

We were still going forward, and eventually reached a relatively small room of singular appearance. Imagine a gigantic array of organ-pipes, of every length and thickness. The term was not exact, however, for I quickly perceived that they were not rounded cylinders but sheets of metal, which looked like steel to me. These sheets, standing up on one end, were disposed like the reeds of a set of panpipes, going from the tallest to the shortest and then back up and down again in sequence, thus forming a large number of identical instruments linked in an assembly. In front of these sheets, men armed with little ebonite hammers were striking them in turn. Above the vertical sheets ran metal wires which reminded me strongly of electric telegraph wires, such as we see on our railway lines.

I forgot to note the important point that, as we had come into this room, Jean had rigged both of us out with helmets that enveloped the skull and were exactly fitted to the ears—not solid and resistant metal helmets like those of our ancient knights, but networks of exceedingly close-knit metallic mesh. The workmen were dressed in a similar fashion, and I perceived immediately that, although I could see the ebonite hammers striking the metal sheets—which must have made rounds—I could only perceive a slight, very soft murmur that was not in proportion to the force of the blows.

I tried to speak, but perceived that I could not hear anything. The workers coiffed like us were, however, talking to one another, and I understood that they were reading one another's lips, like our deaf-mutes. I quickly

131

had proof of that, for Jean, looking me full in the face, mutely pronounced a few words, which I translated immediately.

He invited me to follow him, and led me to the back of the workshop, into a small cabin where there was a double lever, suspended from the ceiling and supported by a central stem, from each extremity of which hung a cord. Still talking, but simultaneously supporting the instructions that I did not understand with gestures, he explained to me that I was to take the handle at the extremity of one of these cords in both hands and pull it vigorously toward me; then he did likewise with the other handle, pulling the lever, which forced me to follow its ascendant movement—and alternative and exceedingly simple pattern of movement that only demanded a certain notion of the necessary rhythm. I pulled toward me, and the arm of the lever descended; then I yielded to Jean's effort, which forced it to rise up again, and so on. It was, in fact, the elementary system of the bellows in a forge.

Evidently, it was not necessary to have devoted days and nights to advanced study in order to carry out this rather childish task. Determined to prove my good will, however, and also to pay for my hospitality—which I thought ought not to be prolonged—in the coin demanded of me, I set to work, attentively regulating my actions to those of my companion.

Alas, it was not as easy as I thought. My nerves becoming tangled, my muscles experienced caprices and rebellions, and I had difficulty maintaining the rhythm. Jean patiently operated his handle one-handed, whereas I had great difficulty holding mine in both, while his other hand beat the measure to which I tried to conform. After all, though, I was no more stupid than the next man, and after ten minutes or so the reciprocal movement became chronometric.

Jean congratulated me with a friendly gesture. There was really nothing to it—and I started thinking about other things.

Through the door of the station I could see the others working, moving about and multiplying, and I could not help noticing their zest, and the vivacity and satisfaction of their expressions. Gradually, my thoughts, lulled by the monotony of my task—which was accomplished by a sort of reflex action—took another course.

I thought about the day, perhaps imminent, when I would recount these strange scenes to my astonished compatriots, who would obviously regard them as traveler's tales, entirely invented. Would it not be the same here, if I explained to these foreigners the curiosities of my own Paris? Yes, it would amuse me to tell them how our institutions function—ministries, parliament, elected councils of every sort—but would they believe me? I had, indeed, many things to tell them that, when I thought about them from a distant, seemed implausible.

I don't know whether it was the effect of the manual labor on my brain, but I felt that I had never been endowed with a more vivid perception or a more active imagination. My mind was liberated and elevated. A desire was born within me to do something useful, and I began to plan out a book in which I would compare the Paris of the Gobi to the Paris in France…

There was a violent shock; I had lost the rhythm! Already, however, Jean had repaired the mistake and we were getting under way again…

Then my companion said—and mimed—that the task was finished; two comrades came in who took our places and began operating the lever. I paused briefly to watch them, but Jean passed his arm through mine and led me away.

In another room we took off our helmets, and stowed them away in a little cupboard. Save for the material, they were reminiscent of the headphones of telephone operators. I made a careful note of the number of my locker in order to make no mistake the following day.

"Well," Jean asked me, "what do you think of that labor?"

"What, pulling that cord?" I said, disdainfully. "In truth, if you call that labor…and for that duration…"

"I thought you did superbly, you know. You pulled the cord for more than an hour."

"Bah! I thought it was ten minutes at the most."

"A full hour, you may be sure. And you can take it from me that, seeing that you were getting a taste for it, I would have let you work longer if my responsibility had not been too seriously engaged."

"What responsibility?"

"The risk of death."

"What?" I said, with a start.

"No one should remain at that post for more than an hour. You were unaware of the danger, but we know it. However strong one might be, one cannot protect oneself against a certain anguish that acts over time upon the nervous system…"

"Come on, you're joking. You're not claiming that in performing those maneuvers we were running some danger…"

"Yes, while avoiding others. It's the truth. For you to understand that, though, it's necessary that you be fully informed about our industrial methods. We have an hour before we go to the Louvre—if you'd like me to,

I'll introduce you to the director of the phonic factory—the phonatery, as we call it. He'll be better able than I am to tell you about the astonishing problems that we've solved."

"Let's go," I said, resolutely. I followed him with a firm step, experiencing a certain price in thinking that I had—albeit without being aware of it—occupied a particularly perilous post. We would see tomorrow that I was not a coward. So I now knew that I had earned the right to material life by risking my life, that I owed nothing to anyone and that I had no need to worry about the cares of existence. It had its good points.

While I was reflecting—declaring myself very satisfied with my performance—young Jean had followed a corridor that had led us to a staircase hollowed out in the rock. We went up thirty steps and found ourselves in an office in which, seated at a desk striped by numerous pigeon-holes, the director—Monsieur Henri Morel—was writing in his ledger.

Jean introduced me. Monsieur Morel studied me attentively. "Then you come from...the other world?" he said to me, in a courteous tone.

"The real world, if you please," I said, trifle piqued. "The one that surrounds you in every direction and from which you are so unfortunately separated."

He started laughing heartily. "Believe me, I had no intention of insulting you. I could, however, engage you in debate regarding that adjective, *unfortunately*. Before anything else, though, how may I help you?"

Jean explained our request. I was totally ignorant of the science of this other world and we begged the eminent director to be so kind as to give me a succinct but clear account that would permit me to understand...the incomprehensible.

"I am at your disposal," said the amiable scientist. "I merely ask you for permission to keep an eye on things while I explain."

"Don't put yourself out, I beg you—if you would rather postpone the conversation…"

"Not at all. As I say, I'm at your disposal."

Henri Morel settled himself comfortably in his arm-chair. He was about fifty years old, with a ruddy face. He had certainly not been harmed by the gazo-mineral dietary regime. "You know, I presume," he began, "how our forefathers were cast by the wickedness of men and the convulsions of nature into this desert, where they found themselves imprisoned. You're not unaware of the terrible living circumstances to which we were reduced. The primary desire, in the panic of the catastrophe, was to flee—but how could the wall of rock surrounding us be penetrated?

"It's evident that for long years, before resigning themselves to their isolation, our unfortunate ancestors had no other thought but to open an exit in the direction of the fatherland that was lost to them forever. They fashioned stone tools, of which we have discovered specimens. What could those wretched instruments do against those masses of basalt and granite? And yet, we have found the vestiges if a very long tunnel they had begun, which remains as testimony to their energy and perseverance.

"Later, having failed with percussion tools, they installed rotatory machines that communicated a rapid movement to drills—but the tips broke; human effort, continuous and exhausting, could not give the drills the necessary rotatory velocity. It was then that one of them, in quest of a motive force, remembered the teachings of

Denis Papin and the theories he published regarding the utilization of steam.

"It has to be remembered, too, that we only had available to the contents of our little interior lake—which almost dried out completely in summer. Even so, at the risk of very rapidly running out of the primary material, people set to work constructing a sort of stone boiler, hermetically sealed, save for one point that was sealed in a less resistant manner and fitted with a sort of cork. It must have been very rudimentary. Ill-designed and ill-constructed—but perhaps one day, out of simple curiosity, we'll go back to that ancient experiment.

"The boiler was filled with water and heated intensively. What happened—as might easily have been predicted—was that the valve did not work, and the container burst under the interior pressure, with a frightful noise of an astonishing shrillness. There were casualties—dead and wounded—but one of the people who had witnessed the experiment had noticed something odd, which was that an old windmill that was more than a thousand paces away from the explosive apparatus had started to turn without any apparent cause, at prodigious speed.

"That man was named Gaspard Meunier; he was a dreamer whose imagination often drew him beyond realities, but whose faculty of intuition was in some ways superhuman. That fact—the gyration of the windmill—to which no one else had paid any heed, became the departure point of his research, and the day came when he affirmed that the seemingly-inexplicable movement had not been produced by the agitation of the air in consequence of the explosion but by the sound that had been emitted…"

From this point on I shall have to translate the worthy Henri Morel's explanation into current language; naturally, he employed the scientific phraseology of his own country, which is fundamentally analogous to, but different in form from, our ordinary terminology. Meunier had first discovered that sound was the result of mathematically numbered vibrations, and that the numbers in question, relative to the pitch, loudness and quality of the sound, would inscribe themselves on sheets of mica sprinkled with sand. Among us, if I'm not mistaken, Chladni[23] published his treatise on acoustics in 1809 or thereabouts, and our students of physics are quite familiar with the square plates of glass on which, in response to the action of a violin bow, particles of sand "write" the note emitted as a sort of hieroglyph.

Meunier, however, went much further; he wondered whether, since the sound displaced the sand, it might constitute a motor in its own right, and whether, if he succeeded in discovering the modalities of its action, analyzed them and contrived their control, he would be able to produce combined, continuous or alternating displacements by the appropriate generation of sound—which, communicated to engines *ad hoc*, might be transformed into movements of any sort.

He had then made two important discoveries. The first was that a body set in vibration can communicate to another body, without contact, movements that can provoke the disintegration of matter. Thus, windows are

---

[23] Ernst Chladni (1756-1827) actually published his treatise *Die Akustic* [Acoustics] in 1802, but the experiment cited here was first carried out by Robert Hooke in 1680; Chladni's version was reported in his *Entdeckungen über die Theorie des Klanges* [Discoveries in the Theory of Sound] (1787).

sometimes broken by the sound of musical instruments, and the human voice can make a glass resonate and break. The second was that our ears can only perceive sound within the limits of a certain scale, between 32 and 73,700 vibrations per second, and he became convinced that the motive force of sound resided in notes not perceptible to our ears—which is to say, formed by a number of vibrations superior to 73,700.

Meunier established, no longer auditively but mechanically, the real existence of these unexpected sounds, which he called "mute sounds" or *hypersons*, constituted by hundreds of thousands of vibrations—and he had the joy, and the glory, in capturing these mute sounds, whether produced by blasts, the friction of a bow or by percussion on ultra-vibrant materials, of discovering and creating phonic mechanics from scratch.

One fact materialized that nearly put a permanent stop to this research, however: in the margin between perceptible vibrations and those of mute sound—which is to say, between 73,700 and 73,800 vibrations, there are notes that determine the disruption of the human auditory organs and, furthermore, the disintegration of the brain. It is only beyond 73,800 that the human apparatus loses its sensibility—and the passage from sensibility to insensibility is a zone so dangerous that it constitutes a mortal peril.

Numerous accidents occurred when Meunier apparatus gradually raised the pitch of sound to the point of rendering it inaudible—and yet, the mechanical action only began beyond that zone, which it was necessary to surpass.

An observation might be made here: these theories, extraordinary as they might appear, reminded me of those that have recently been revealed by the discovery of invisible light—X-rays, N-rays, etc.[24]

To return to Meunier's studies, however, it was to ward off these dangers that the great man, who had begun to despair of success, had suddenly invented the *parason*: the metallic mesh of which the preservative helmet was fabricated, with which the workmen were equipped, and which plays with respect to the dangerous notes the same role as the metallic curtain of a Davy lamp vis-à-vis the flame and firedamp.

That explained to me why, during the sinister scene of the Phonothanatos, I was the only person whose ears were uncovered, while young Isabelle, plying her bow over her cithara, had strayed over the limits of the mortiferous zone, delaying the murderous note—the inaudible note that would have killed me—with all her skill!

How much time and patience it must have required to study mineral bodies and metals from the viewpoint of the possible production of these hypersons! But what magnificent results had been achieved!

The phonic factory in which I had worked that morning was a great generator of motive force by means of sound. The sheets that I had seen in action generated sounds, of which the highest in pitch—inaudible—

---

[24] N-Rays were "discovered" by René Blondlot in 1802, and the discovery confirmed by more than a hundred other scientists, but some of those who could not detect them commissioned Robert Wood to investigate, and his report that Blondlot claimed to see the N-rays even when the prism had been secretly removed from his apparatus convinced the world at large that the whole affair had been an error. Lermina presumably completed his story before Blondlot was discredited.

reached a figure of 35,184,372,088,832 vibrations: 35,184 billion movements per second.

And, in spite of these incalculable numbers, was it not easy to comprehend that such an intensity of move-ment—which defies imagination—could be communi-cated to matter, and to turbines rotting at 622,000 cycles per second, which, fitted to incredibly resistant drills, could perforate the hardest rock, pulverize stone and dis-integrate granite?

Chemistry had done the rest.

I was curious to know what role the lever that I had operated that morning with my friend Jean played in the factory. It was a sonic ventilator that prevented the ac-cumulation of dangerous notes in the workshops: a sort of lightning-conductor, which prevented others being stuck down but could—I shuddered!—strike down those operating it.

Sound could be transformed into heat and light! The seemingly-electric bulbs were illuminated by music!

Thus, these disinherited exiles, ignorant of all our progress, had discovered a force that rendered them the same services as steam and electricity.

"And soon," said a voice behind me, "we shall have a force a thousand times more powerful at our disposal!"

I saw the worthy Morel shudder, and a singular fleeting expression passed over his face—something like repulsion, almost wrathful terror. He mastered himself immediately, though. "Oh, it's you, Monsieur Henri Lévêque. What can I do for you?"

I turned round and looked at the newcomer. He was a man of about 30, with a long face and thin lips. His eyes, deeply sunken beneath an exceedingly bulbous forehead, were small, but they were so bright that it was difficult to sustain their gaze.

I cannot say whether the impression that singular physiognomy made on me was sympathetic or antipathetic, but it was very keen and very deep; one sensed that one was confronted by an exceptional energy.

"Monsieur Henri Morel, I need to talk to you about an important subject, and I have come to ask you if you would grant me a hearing at the Louvre during the meal."

Morel—this time I was certain of it—made a gesture of protest; he wanted to refuse. His courtesy, however—or some other sentiment—triumphed over his private inclinations. "I refuse nothing," he said. "Moreover, since the time has come to go to the Louvre, we can all go together, if you wish."

As we followed the quay of the florid Seine, I whispered in Jean's ear: "Well, either I don't know my physiognomy, or these two fellows—Morel and Lévêque—are, if not enemies, at least rivals. But on what ground?"

My friend signaled to me to lower my voice; then, forcing me to step up the pace, he said to me in a grave, almost sad tone: "You've guessed it. Between these two men, the gravest interests of the Republic are at stake—a terrible conflict of parties…"

"What? Do you have political disputes, then?"

"I don't have time to explain, but if you overhear any argument—and I don't doubt that one will burst forth—beware of becoming involved in it. The Grand Châtelet might not have said its final word."

"At least tell me whether you're on Morel's side or Lévêque's."

"I don't know," he replied.

I looked at him. He was a trifle pale.

In spite of myself, I felt a tightness in my chest. I glanced surreptitiously at Henri Lévêque. Very calmly, but with an expression of tenacity that tautened all the muscles in his face, he was walking alongside Morel without speaking to him.

We arrived at the Louvre.

XI.

Scarcely had I entered the palace of alimentation when my eyes spontaneously sought out the lovely Isabelle.

In fact, I now had a better understanding of the right that she had to my gratitude; she had quite literally saved my life, when the cruel judges of the High Court had condemned me to death. And what courage it must have required! For humanity's sake, she had exposed herself to the harshest punishment, and it was at the risk of her own existence that she had delayed the emission of the note that would have killed me. I had not yet rendered her sufficient testimony of my gratitude. When I spotted her, I hurried toward her. She was in the midst of a group of young women who, observing my impatience, began to laugh maliciously—but Isabelle politely came toward me, extending her hand.

I told her, in a slightly tremulous voice, how glad I was to see her again, asked her, politely, whether her morning's work had wearied her.

"Wearied?" she exclaimed. "Not at all! My morning labor is, as for everyone else, an exercise in hygienic gymnastics that does us a great deal of good—but I've heard that you have been working too, at the Phonatery."

"Indeed," I said, lightly. "I assisted my friend Jan to operate the ventilator."

"The ventilator! Such a dangerous post! Oh, that's very good." Her eyes were fixed on mine with a tenderness whose sincerity was slightly embarrassing—for, in truth, I had been unaware of the peril I had faced.

Fortunately, Jean came to me rescue. "Our friend will do his three days," he said, "like everyone else—after which we shall let him choose a task in accordance with his tastes."

"Have, you, then, decided to take up permanent residence among us?" Isabelle asked.

An amiable gallantry came to my lips, but I reminded myself that our Parisian whimsies were inappropriate here. I contented myself with affirming that everything in this unknown country seemed interesting to me, and that my greatest desire was to learn everything there was to know about its institutions and mores—to which another young woman with a pretty face replied: "We would also like to know what is going on in your Paris. You'll tell us, won't you?"

"Later!" Jean interjected. "If you wish, Mesdemoiselles, we shall rejoin you for dessert, and you can interrogate our guest at your leisure."

"Yes, yes! Do that!" cried numerous voices. "How amusing it will be!"

I addressed my kindest regards to everyone—and to Isabelle in particular—and followed Jean Lefèvre to the table that I already considered as mine because I had occupied it the day before. It is quite true that nothing is easier to acquire than a habit.

A vague anxiety was haunting me, however. "Tell me," I whispered in Jean's ear, "did I commit some breach of correctness just now by introducing myself into the group that included my gracious executioner?"

"What breach of correctness?"

"The last thing I would want is to compromise her..."

"I don't quite understand," Jean replied, laughing. "Presumably you fear injuring her reputation..."

"That's it, exactly."

"Well, be assured that such ideas are not current here; we live, girls and boys alike, in absolute comradeship. If a particular affection awakens between two people, they submit of their own free will to the experiment of the hematometer…"

"What?"

"It's a measuring device of the greatest interest, according to which marriages are decided."

"What? Technological marriages?" I said, I a mocking tone.

Jean shrugged his shoulders carelessly. "All right! I don't suppose you have any desire to get married as yet. Let's leave it at that. Take your place—and if you're anything of a psychologist, observe attentively what is happening around us."

I installed myself in front of my elementary piano; I took from its case the amber tip that I had been given as a symbol and instrument of my right to life, earned by my labor and, like a virtuoso before his Pleyel,[25] I deciphered my first course with a finger that gradually became more confident.

In our floral booth I recognized the serious men that I had encountered the day before, and rediscovered Henri Morel, whom I had not noticed in my initial, quite natural, excitement. Facing him was Henri Lévêque, who, being part of another company, had been oblige to solicit an invitation. Including Jean and myself, there were a dozen people in all.

---

[25] A piano made under the supervision of Ignatz Pleyel (1757-1831) or his son Camille (1788-1895), who inherited the family business.

At the beginning of the meal there was a certain tension in the air. Everyone was sitting stiffly in his seat, sucking his chibouk like an earnest Ottoman.

During the second course, Henri Morel—whose position as director of the Phonatery gave him a considerable importance—decided to get started on the conversation. "Monsieur Henri Lévêque," he said, "you have requested an interview, and I have put myself at your disposal, with my friends. We are listening, if you please." The formulas were courteous, nothing more.

Henri Lévêque frowned, his eyebrows forming two black and heavily emphasized arches beneath the astonishing protuberance of his forehead. It seems to me that he was simultaneously gathering all his patience and all his thoughts.

"I thank you for your kindness," he said, in a rather dry tone. "I shall try not to abuse it. I ask your permission, however, to recap from the beginning the history of the discovery that constitutes the reason and justification for the observations I need to submit to you."

He did so; I shall summarize his explanation as briefly as possible.

By virtue of long and patient experiments, Henri Lévêque had established the following facts.

Odorant materials—the perfumes of which are perceived at a distance by the olfactory nerves, and some of which are endowed with an invasive property that nothing can resist—continually give off particles of their own substance; these particles are infinitesimal in dimension and are numbered in billions.

It had been known for a long time that a grain of musk emits 57 million particles in 24 hours without its weight diminishing perceptibly—an illusion due, in any case, to the imperfection of the instruments. That is what

William Crookes, in our Occident, has called "molecular bombardment."

Without being familiar with that expression, Henry Lévêque had verified the fact, which he had designated by the Greek-derived term Aromapiezia—from *aroma*, perfume, and *piesis*, compression, the latter part embodying a new observation, reputedly of genius. He had determined that the perpetual and vertiginous projection of particles in question could be controlled, checked and channeled, and was constituted by the compression and expansion of a force of incalculable power.

Remembering Papin's invention, he had constructed an aromatic boiler, a sort of hollow shell, the principle of which consisted of the incarceration in the interior of a solid block of a substance productive of perfumed particles. The shell had been sealed hermetically and put in a safe place in order that any serious accident might be avoided.

Eight years had elapsed since the construction of the aromatic shell, and no one had thought any more about it until the population had been woken up one morning by a frightful detonation. The shell had burst under the enormous pressure that the molecules amassed inside it, and accumulated over such a long time, had exercised upon the walls, and the explosion had been so violent that the granite had been pulverized to such an extent that it had scarcely been possible to find the shards of the machine.

The demonstration was complete. Perfume was merely one mode of action of the centrifugal force embodied in every terrestrial substance.

Henri Lévêque, who had been mocked pitilessly, had resumed work. He had found a means of activating the dissociation of particles, while regulating the process. Compressed aroma gradually revealed all of its expansive power, which turned out to be ten times that of sound—3000 meters per second instead of 300—and an initial machine was constructed, which was applied to the elevator known as the aromal claw and which, by virtue of the configuration of the country was, if I might put it thus, the *Métropolitain par excellence*.

An aromatic motor occupied a much more restricted space than a phonic motor. Furthermore, the study of odorant materials had revealed that all odors, without exception, are derived from one primal perfume, the principle of which resides in schists and asphalts, all other perfumes being merely different combinations of that elementary perfume.

Henri Lévêque established that perfume is a radiation of matter, and manifests itself by vibrations that are not more numerous than those of sound and light but—and this was the vital point of the great inventor's discoveries—but rhythmic in a different way, without isochronism: the pendular regularity of alternating movements that had until then been regarded as inherent in all manifestations of movement. Perfume operated in syncopation.

I shall not linger over these technical subtleties. In brief, Henri Lévêque had discovered substances emitting between 50 and a million particles a second. It is easy to understand that the impact of these particles produces such a pressure on the wall of an apparatus or the organs that are adapted to it that it produces mechanical effects whose power terrifies the imagination.

Thus, Henri Lévêque had isolated the principles of this new science, had discovered the primal matter and, finally, had developed its effects to the maximum.

He had now constructed a machine in which the perfume—the aroma—played the dual role of motor and instrument. Compressed by certain methods—which he promised to reveal to a specially-appointed commission—the aroma acquired such a proportionate force that the particles, forming, so to speak, a bullet, could penetrate mineral and metallic masses to an extraordinary depth, piercing them and disintegrating them a hundred times more rapidly that steel drills with diamond tips, however solid and sharp they might be imagined to be. These bores could be effected at a rate of 40 meters—I am using our measures for the sake of clarity—per second.

"The results that I have already obtained," said Henri Lévêque, will confirm the reality of what I have just told you. Thus, to sum up, with the aid of my aromal tools, I can pierce and disintegrate mineral or metallic masses several leagues thick in a matter of hours: a gigantic effort of which—don't take this the wrong way, Monsieur Henri Morel—the most formidable of your phonic engines would be incapable."

Henri Lévêque got up then, his eyes sparkling, and as he did so, he made an expansive gesture that seemed to embrace the horizon beyond the walls of the Louvre. "I affirm that by means of the aromapiezia and the machines that have been constructed in my workshops, nothing is easier that to break the wall of rocks, mountains and granite and metallic masses that surround us, almost instantaneously, thus to put ourselves in communication with the world from which we might have been separated by horrible catastrophes, but which we have not forgotten, and is not foreign to us…"

There was a stir in the crowd.

Jean, who was sitting next to me, took my hand and squeezed it as if to crush it.

A profound silence fell.

I understood that the orator had touched a vital subject. His voice had risen, becoming loud and vibrant, almost solemn.

"You know," he continued, that our forefathers, more than 150 years ago, had the ambition—the passion, I ought to say—of breaking down the wall that was stifling them, of clearing a passage through it. A few paces from here we have recovered the traces of a tunnel that they tried to dig through the granite. After ten years of effort, they had to renounce that exhausting labor, which they judged futile. Immured they were, immured they would remain.

"That was a moment of despair, which followed a period of depression, and then of resignation. They abandoned all hope, all dreams of escape, and no longer thought of anything but survival. They renounced everything—the fatherland, and humankind! Yes, they survived, but in an egotistical and debilitating isolation.

"Have those times of resignation and cowardice not long gone? Have not former generations whose consciousness was beaten down by the blows of misfortune be succeeded by a new race that needs air, space and liberty—which wants to re-enter the human brotherhood? That new race knows that beyond these enormous barriers there are people similar to us, who work, think and act, and who, far from confining themselves to the egotistical enjoyment of an enervating well-being, exchange ideas and hopes with all the Earth's inhabitants!

"Perhaps, far from here, science and industry are less advanced than ours! Perhaps technology and chemistry are still in an embryonic state, and the progress of which we are so proud has not been realized. Is it not our duty to bring those people the fruit of our mediations and our labor?

"I shall conclude. I have discovered aromapiezia. Let that invention mark for us a new era: that of liberation, escape, of our re-entry into universal life. Let the will of you all encourage me! Let your aspirations for living space, for the terrestrial immensity, for these people who are your kindred, be my auxiliaries, and within a month you shall be free!

"I have spoken. Decide!"

Tempestuous applause was unleashed. One might have thought that Henri Lévêque's words had awoken thoughts latent in all those brains, which had suddenly sprung forth in a cry of enthusiasm. I thought at first that it was public opinion.

I was very soon disabused; with acclamations and protests were mingled jeers and cries of anger—and then I guessed why Henri Morel, the knight of phonism, had so much difficulty hiding his antipathy toward the inventor of aromism.

They were definitely more than rivals; they were enemies—sworn enemies—and I had the proof of that when Henri Morel, drawing himself up to his full height, and having put a little device to his mouth that I later discovered to be a phonomultiplier of his own invention, shouted in a mighty voice that drowned the tumult and made the mica windows tremble: "Beware, people! People, you are being deceived! Don't let yourselves be won over by cunning words! People, do not abandon your happy reality for illusory dreams! What? Have you forgotten that your kindred fled from persecutions, the memory of which makes us shudder. What? You have happiness and leisure, you enjoy a social organization that sets you free, rid of any material and moral care—and you would renounce all that?

"Do you not know that there is perpetual war in the old world? And you have peace? There is poverty—and you have well-being! And you will obey the suggestions of this man, whose genius I do not deny, but whose feverish ambitions I denounce! What he wants is glory, for noise to be made around his inventions—the honorific rewards that we disdain, but with which other men are prodigal!

"To satisfy these evil aspirations—which he endows with the fine pretext of universal fraternity—he will deliver you, the pacifists, to murderous wars, you, the fortunate, to the struggle for existence. No! No! You must not listen to appeals that tend to the destruction of the work so patiently elaborated by your forefathers. Remain the custodians of these marvels that are your protection, the guarantees of your independence, of your happiness, of your future!

"Think, if you listen to this man, what a responsibility you are assuming on behalf of your children!"

Suddenly, public opinion was reversed.

"Yes, yes!" the cry went up. "Down with Lévêque! Hurrah for Morel! Down with aroma! Hurrah for sound!"

Henri Lévêque stood there impassively, with his arms folded over his chest and his head held high, utterly obstinate.

When Morel, doubtless sure of his victory, sat down amid frantic applause, Doctor Durand gave him the accolade. It was a triumph! The isolationist cause seemed to be won.

Lévêque merely said: "I shall remain alone in the breach, which I shall not surrender! Truth is on the march; it will overturn all obstacles."

Quarrels and altercations were now breaking out in every part of the room. The aromists—and they still formed a significant minority—were taking the phonists to task, calling them egotistical, backward-looking and self-satisfied. To which the phonists were replying by calling the aromists traitorous and unpatriotic.

"They've sold out to humanity!" one voice cried out.

The cacophony became terrible. The specter of civil war loomed.

Then Jean Lefèvre—whose emotion was visible—climbed on to his chair and shouted in his shrill voice that he had a motion to propose.

As he was extremely popular among the young, he was applauded, which prevented him from speaking. Very impartially, however—it must be admitted—Henri Morel took a flask of compressed sound from his pocket and opened it. It released an enormous noise into the assembly, a sort of roar like a gigantic ship's siren. It was, it seemed, a kind of presidential gavel.

Everyone fell silent, stunned and nonplussed.

After a few minutes of calming down, Jean Lefèvre was able to explain himself.

He was not taking sides either with those who wanted to remain confined forever within their walls, nor for the adventurous spirits that were reaming of an entry into the civilized world. He was proposing both the nomination of a committee of enquiry and a plebiscite.

What was the external world in which it was proposed they should take their place? That, after all, was what it was necessary to know. Now, a unique and unexpected opportunity had presented itself to obtain precise information: it was the presence of an inhabitant of that unknown world, of the young stranger beside him, Alcide Trémalet, so honest and likeable (it is Jean who is speaking), and who might be invited to speak at a series of conferences about the industrial, social and intellectual condition of these mysterious regions...

After that, all the inhabitants would be consulted about the decision to be made.

The inquiry would, of course, be contradictory and the allegations of the speaker would be subjected to a rain of criticism, but for now, the phonists and aromists agreed to accept the resolution dictated by the great voice of the people...

Any proposition for the nomination of a committee is readily taken up by any assembly. It is a practical procedure for, ordinarily, postponing a question indefinitely—a parliamentary one that satisfies the hesitant, calms the impatient and delights the indolent.

"Yes, yes! The committee! Hurrah for Alcide Trémalet!"

People addressed themselves to me. I became an important person. Henri Morel asked me whether I would accept the mission of which the confidence of the people judged med worthy. Emotionally, I put my hand on my heart,

Isabelle had sidled toward our group, and her gaze told me to make the vow.

"Citizens," I said, modestly. "I am at your disposal."

I was appointed as a lecturer—and, as is only just, I was applauded.

XII.

It is without vanity—take my word for it—that I affirm here the great, the very great, success of my talks. I am not absolutely eloquent, but my speech is pleasing. People were also very keen to hear what I had to say, and for more than a fortnight I held my audience spellbound.

Anyway, was there any subject vaster or finer?

What a splendid image is that of our civilizations developing through catastrophes without number! Wars, especially, excited my audience; with what brio I recounted the campaigns of Louis XIV, the triumphs of the Republican armies, the Napoleonic epic...a triumphal march that strewed all the road of Europe with cadavers! When I told them about the horrors of the Berezina, there was a delirious response.[26] The hall was breathless. Never until then had they had any inkling of such anguish. Those naïve and innocent souls savored fear, disgust and horror.

Isabelle said to me: "I've never wept before! How content I am!"

Unknown sentiments awoke among my listeners; they became exited, brandishing their fists at unknown enemies.

Then, elevating myself to the great heights of economic science, I spoke about the miseries so valiantly borne by the masses, and told them about the joys of

---

[26] The Berezina is a Russian river, over which the retreating French army passed between November 26 and 29 1812, continually harassed by the enemy.

charity, a miracle of generosity. "We no longer have more than 500,000 poor people in Paris! Within a century, that figure will be reduced by at least ten per cent!"

They drank up my words, to the letter.

What surprised me disagreeably, I must say, was to learn that Monsieur Henri Morel, obedient to the sentiments of a base jealousy, had instituted a lecture course contradictory to my own, in which he raised a more than malevolent criticism of the civilization of which I was painting such a magnificent picture, condemning us as barbarians, contrasting our life, so intense and so combative, with the soft placidity of his closed city.

For his part, though, Monsieur Henri Lévêque was extremely busy. Outside the hours of labor—which were being reduced by the day—the Paris of the Orient was no longer anything but a closed arena in which the most starkly contrasted opinions collided with one another and grabbed one another by the hair (do opinions have hair?). People insulted one another, raked one another with their nails, and slandered one another. The city had finally come to life!

I had finally decided to take the side of the aromists. Listening to myself speak, I had convinced myself. Although I had initially been inclined to admire the sonic system, thanks to which nothing was lacking, I could not admit that the theories dear to my beloved fatherland were shameful. So I had to put more ardor into my demonstrations.

It was among women, especially, that my propaganda obtained the best results. I had found lyrical terms in which to paint for them the marvels of our great capitals, in the first rank of which I naturally placed our Paris, and through a distant mirage I took them for an excursion through our boulevards, our avenues, our

Champs-Elysées, our Bois de Boulogne. They saw themselves sprawling nonchalantly in carriages drawn by prize horses, wrapped in silks and smiling at cavaliers of distinction. Or I evoked the halls of the Opéra, the Comédie-Française and generic theaters, and they were enraptured with delight on hearing the artistes that I mimicked to perfection. It was one of my most pleasing social gifts. Mounet-Sully was acclaimed, Coquelin called back for an encore. As for the great Sarah, all the women attempted to recover her golden voice.[27] I sketched types and costumes on a blackboard. Feet were stamped.

Isabelle was transformed; I surprised her declaiming verses by Corneille; she talked about dyeing her hair and had concocted a bolero in laminated zinc. I could not resist her seductions any longer, and I asked her whether she would consent to unite her destiny with mine.

"Will you take me back to your homeland?" she asked.

What will one not promise when one is in love?

We confided our plan to Doctor Durand and my young friend Jean Lefèvre, who gave us their approval. "Nothing else remains," the latter said to me, "than to submit yourselves to the preliminary formality of the hematometer."

I made enquiries; this was the result. The word—of Greek origin again—signifies the measurement of blood. According to the laws of that bizarre country, unions were only authorized between individuals whose blood was in harmony.

---

[27] The "great Sarah" was Sarah Bernardt (1844-1923). The tragedian who used the stage name Mounet-Sully (Jean-Sully Mounet, 1841-1916) was one of her lovers.

When the mechanism of the hematometer was demonstrated to me, I recognized the principle of an instrument commonly employed in certain physiological experiments: the sphygmograph, or recorder of pulse-beats. These pulsations can be inscribed in a graphic form, specimens of which can be seen in various scientific treatises. A calm pulse produces an expression like a leisurely wave, whereas an agitated pulse produced a much more jagged formation.

The hematometer registers the pulsations of the entire body, by means of procedures that would take too long to describe, but whose graphic result is analogous to that of the sphygmograph—except that it gives a more complete result of the intimate movements of the entire organism. One can only marry a person whose graph is compatible with one's own, with a maximum discrepancy of five millimeters. This ensures that the two spouses are guaranteed against physiological or cerebral contrasts, from which the quarrels that are the bane of households are born.

Isabelle and I conformed graphically, to the millimeter! And we were married.

It was happiness. It was a radiant future.

More than a month has passed since I last picked up my pen—a soft vulture-quill, which sits well in the hand. What would I have had to write about during that time? Happiness has no history, and I would only have been able to conjugate and reconjugate the verb: I am happy.

I must confess that I have completely neglected my course of lectures. Has not chatting *à deux* with my dear Isabelle been sufficient?

Every day, of course, I accomplished my national task, which now consisted of crushing mineral specimens for two hours a day. At first I had been set to wash mica tiles, but it appeared that I was far from having the requisite aptitude.

When I had paid my debt of labor, I confess that I imitated the lizard that warms itself slothfully in the sun. My wife and I went joyfully to the National Refectory, where we had reserved a delightfully solitary corner. Then we walked, hand in hand, along the banks of the Florescent Seine, or spent a few hours at the concert hall or the theater. I saw *Le Cid* ten times.[28]

It was an exquisite life, exempt from all cares.

Toward the latter part of the month, however, I observed that the lovely Isabelle seemed somewhat preoccupied; she stifled sighs and her gaze was veiled by an inexplicable sadness. I questioned her tentatively, but she avoided any direct response.

"What's wrong, my darling?"

"Nothing, my love."

That dialogue, which is translatable into any language, is familiar throughout the world.

Some days ago, under the pretext of some supplementary labor, she abandoned me for a few hours in the afternoon; when she came back, I noticed an unaccustomed agitation. I kept quiet and observed; I knew that a woman always talks eventually—as, of course, she did. One evening, as of obedient to a force more powerful than her will, she drew me to her, embraced me and said; "You're going to take me to your homeland, aren't you?"

When I exhibited some surprise, she told me that the agitation provoked by Henri Lévêque, to the main-

_____

[28] The Corneille tragedy of 1636, whose title was appropriated for application to any intrepid and gallant young warrior.

tenance and overexcitement of which I had made a considerable personal contribution by means of my excellent lectures, had only increased. The enquiry set up to compare the situation of the Asiatic Paris with that of the European Paris had yielded decisive results; my homeland had carried off the laurels everywhere. The theories of the aromists—the will to rejoin the universal course of affairs—had gained so much ground that the success of Henri Lévêque in the plebiscite that was to take place the following day was no longer in doubt.

"And we shall leave here, my husband, my darling husband!" Isabelle warbled, clapping her hands. "And your little wifey will make tours of the lake and the Bois de Boulogne in a carriage, with pretty, pretty costumes and large hats…like this!"

She flung her arms wide in a theatrical gesture.

Strangely enough, that idea—returning to my homeland—did not cause me as much satisfaction as I had expected. I scarcely dared to confess to myself that I found myself very comfortable in this lost Paris, whose peacefulness and security enchanted me. I knew full well that, back there, I would find my friends again—pooh! Here, I had contrived a charming hearth, habits and distractions for myself. I had even taught my friend Jean *manille*.[29]

Back there, I would have shares, and an annual income—but here I had no need of them. I did not even have any anxieties regarding the devaluation of currencies, the sinking of Panamas,[30] everyday bankruptcies—

---

[29] *Manille* is a card game—but the word is also used to mean an anklet, or a shackle.

[30] Shares in the long-delayed Panama Canal became a by-word in France for disastrous investments.

there was no Bourse! I lived without anxiety for the morrow.

Isabelle's enthusiasm alarmed me slightly; launched into the whirlwind of Parisian society, would she be any happier? Discreetly, I murmured a few objections in her ear.

"Tell me straight out if you're breaking your promise," she said, not without a certain bitterness.

"No, certainly not, but…"

"Or if you've lied to us in describing the marvels of your Parisian civilization."

"Oh, as to that, I swear…"

"Are you determined that your wife will always wear sheet metal dresses?"

I lowered my head. That was when I found out that the plebiscite that would determine the fate of the Republic was to take place the following day.

"And the aromists will win!" cried Isabelle. "I'll put my shirt on it!" As you can see, I had already initiated her into the mysteries of our language. "We'll have a large majority," she concluded, "of which I understand that you will be part." And she added, in a severe tone: "I'll take you to vote myself!"

Without further discussion, I went to find my friends Lefèvre and Durand. They were very preoccupied, and had not yet made up their minds which way to vote.

The doctor, by virtue of his age, was more sympathetic to the conservative ideas of Henri Morel. "Since we've always been so happy," he said, "why take the risk?"

"Can we remained buried forever?" Jean objected. "Is there not within us, in spite of all arguments, an in-

162

stinct that can only be satisfied by re-entry into the universal course of affairs."

"And what if we expose ourselves to new dangers, new sources of anguish?"

"There'll always be time to exile ourselves again," Jean relied. "Would it be so difficult to recover our solitude?"

I was no less perplexed. For the first time, I realized the responsibility that I had assumed. In the depths of my consciousness, I greatly appreciated the peace that I enjoyed here. I knew perfectly well, myself, to what hazards Occidental civilization would expose these good people. I sketched out a few objections, one of which struck them quite forcibly.

I admitted that the wall could be pierced, that they could escape from the enclosed city—but where would they be? In the middle of the desert. Three thousand human beings lost in the wilderness of the Gobi. Which way would they head? Toward China? I have been obliged to flee from a massacre there. Toward Tibet? The Lamas were more ferocious persecutors than the Boxers! And if they could not manage to reach a civilized country in reasonable time, what would the fate of their caravan be? Were they not risking a frightful death by fatigue and privations of every sort?

"What about chemico-alimentary tablets?" Jean replied. "We'll be able to force a passage through those barbarian hordes!"

The doctor shook his head. He told me than that the phonists—the supporters of the *status quo*—were determined to oppose the exodus by any means possible, including force.

"But what if the plebiscite gives a majority to the aromists?"

"Will they submit to its decision? I doubt it."

"They'd dare to resist the will of the people?"

"It's quite possible."

"What! A *coup d'état!*"

Durand did not reply, but I sensed that he was troubled by grave anxieties.

During the day that preceded the vote, public meetings were opened in every corner of the city. Isabelle left me to go excite the zeal of her companions—for the women, of course, had the same entitlement to vote as the men.

I went to one of the meetings myself. It was a bad move. As soon as I entered the room, I was recognized. The aromists, taking me for one of their most ardent partisans, took possession of me in order to hoist me up to the podium, but the phonists tried to prevent them from doing so; the most ardent grabbed hold of my shoulders and my legs and caused me to fall to the ground. It wouldn't have taken much more for me to break my back.

Henri Lévêque's adherents were determined not to be thwarted, though. They grabbed me back again and, using my body like a catapult, cleared a passage. Finally, the podium was ours. I was stood on my feet, and was eventually able to talk.

What did I say to them? On my honor, I have no idea.

I had no wish to betray my former homeland by associating myself with the acerbic criticisms directed against its beautiful civilization by malevolent individuals, and yet, in all conscience, I could not slander that of the closed city, having tried it out and fund that it suited me admirably—with the result that, attempting to accommodate both the phonist goat and the aromist cabbage, I did not convince anyone…or, at least, so poorly that both parties beat me unmercifully and I was obliged to flee to the conjugal domicile, where I was welcomed by a couple of slaps in the face.

It was the gentle Isabelle that bestowed them upon me. I had betrayed the cause of progress! I had broken all my promises! I was a liar and a traitor!

So much for the hematometer! Our physiologies were certainly not in harmony at that dolorous moment…

I didn't even have the strength to argue. I threw myself on my bed and went to sleep.

When I woke up, I was alone.

I ran to the window. A formidable rumor rose up; I saw people running, jostling one another. On might have thought it was a mob!

It was! At 10 a.m.—I must have slept like a log—the result of the plebiscite had been announced: a majority of more than 1100 for the aromists!

The partisans of Henri More had only received a few more than 800 votes; the others had raised more than 2000.

It was settled. The cause of piercing the mountains had triumphed.

I rushed outside. Where was Isabelle?

The disorder in the streets was indescribable. The people had gone mad. They were demanding that the work of perforation should begin immediately. A dense crowd had invaded Henri Lévêque's workshops and demanded that he put his machines to work there and then.

As if frightened by such a rapid success, he was negotiating, asking for a delay, objecting that his machines were not quite ready. But what could that sage advice achieve in confrontation with the general overexcite-ment? Demagogues, emerged from who knows where, had taken control of the movement. Groups of people were running through the avenues shouting: "To Paris! To Paris!"

A crazy wind was blowing over their heads.

Three o'clock. I'm frightened. The intransigent aromists, fortified by the plebiscite, are demanding the immediate digging of the tunnel. In spite of Henri Lévêque's resistance, they have taken possession of his apparatus, which one of his foremen has agreed to put into action.

Henri Morel has been arrested, and hidden from view. The phonists are determined to release him, at any cost.

Four o'clock. They've succeeded, by means of a bold strike. Henri Morel is free. He has gathered his workers and his partisans, mobilized his machines and set out for the mountains.

Five o'clock. The battle has begun. Frightful deto-nations can be heard; atrocious, discordant, harrowing fanfares testify to the activity of the phonic artillery, while the arrival of gusts of incongruous scents borne by the wind, saturating my nostrils, informs me as to the stubbornness of the aromists.

Who will achieve victory?

Ten past five. I haven't seen Isabelle. I think I glimpsed her a little while ago, though, marching at the head of a company of women, brandishing a standard on which I made out the words: *To Paris! Hurrah for the Bois de Boulogne! Hurrah for the cascade!*

The battle is still going on. Rumor has it that the aromists are gaining ground.

The perfume drills have attacked the mountains in a straight line, and the disintegration is so rapid that the tunnel will be open within an hour. The phonic piercers have been outdistanced. Henri Morel has not given up, though. His most powerful engines have been hoisted up on to the heights and are hollowing out shafts to cut off the tunnel. Entire blocks of several hundred kilograms can be seen breaking up, dissolving and, so to speak, evaporating into the air.

Oh! What's that? I can hear something like the roaring of a torrent! I can see a black column springing up into the sky…terrifying…

I know! I know! It's horrible!

While disembowelling the mountain in every direction, the aromists and phonists have liberated a spring, a lake, a sea of naphtha and bitumen, which, under the pressure of subterranean forces, is gushing into the air and falling back, pouring down on the city!

What an atrocious odor! Under the action of the phonic vibrations, the plutonian minerals have melted, become incandescent and caught fire. They're giving off huge clouds of thick, acrid smoke…and the igneous torrent is flowing down the slope, invading the bed of the florescent Seine…

Everyone's fleeing! But there's no way out—for the mountainous walls on the other side are still intact! The city will be transformed into a lake of burning asphalt! Isabelle! Isabelle!

Here comes someone running, fleeing before the black tide that's pursuing her…

She throws herself into my arms! At least we'll die together!

Ah! A vulture is passing by, dragging its basket behind, whose anchor-line is preventing it from taking off. Courage, Isabelle! Can I get into the basket! Yes?

I throw myself into the gondola, I drag Isabelle into it. I cut the vulture's anchor-rope. It lifts us into the air! Ah! I'm bringing my manuscript with me.

Beneath us, the buildings are melting and collapsing into the black waves.

Fly, vulture, fly! Higher! Higher still!

Isabelle, my sweet Isabelle, shall we ever see the Bois de Boulogne?

Epilogue

This manuscript was found by a *muzhik* in the Bielygrod Plaza in Moscow. It seemed to have fallen from the sky. It reached the hands of the scientists of the University, who thought at first that it was a hoax. After long discussion, however, it was sent to St. Petersburg. There, the ministers convened, and the result of their deliberations—the details of which remain secret—was that an expedition should be sent across the Gobi Desert in search of traces of the mysterious city.

One diplomat said, with all reservations: "If we don't find the city, at least we'll be able to look for a new route to Manchuria."

The Russian expedition has made its report.

No trace of building work has been discovered in the Gobi Desert. However, a layer of bitumen, mingled with pumice and obsidian, extending over a vast area several leagues square, was discovered. This layer, whose thickness is considerable, is evidently of recent formation, for it has not cooled completely. Tools penetrate it with great facility.

Excavations have been started.

It will be understood that the events that have taken place in recent months—the Russo-Japanese war—have deflected attention away from the research, which might be resumed at a later date.

Whatever happens, the oriental Paris—if it ever existed—is a well and truly lost city.

As for Monsieur and Madame Trémalet, they have given no sign of life; nor has the vulture.

TWICE DEAD

I.

Scarcely had I set foot on the soil of France—on my return from a long mission that had kept me in the Far East for three years—than I set out for the corner of the Sologne where my friends were cloistered.

I had once found the idea rather strange of imprisoning oneself with a young woman, almost a child, in a morose solitude, on the day after a marriage of which I would otherwise have strongly approved, by reason of the comradeship that had united the spouses in childhood. I had given them the nicknames Paul and Virginie,[31] and I shall continue to call them that, considering that anonymity is appropriate to the singular facts whose memory I wish to conserve in this story.

Although I am ten years older than Paul, I had always been interested in his character. His excessive nervousness often alarmed me, although, in sum, it did not seem to exercise any bad influence over his actions

---

[31] *Paul et Virginie* (1788) by Jacques Bernardin de Saint-Pierre is one of the classics of French Romanticism, which provided a prototype for a subgenre of tales of intense but doomed love. The narrator's attribution of the names to his two young friends, which ostensibly represents the intensity of their affection for one another, also foreshadows the tragic development of their relationship.

and did not ordinarily manifest itself other than in a rare tenacity of purpose.

I always had a passion for the natural sciences, even before education and circumstance made me the modest savant that I now am, but I have never been endowed with a very good memory. What I lack, in particular, is so-called visual memory. For example, if I encounter some flower I my botanical excursions whose splendor or originality of structure enchants me, it is almost impossible for me, one I am in my study, to reconstruct a cerebral image of the shape or color that delighted me a little while before.

Paul was entirely different. If he happened to be with me when I made the observation, it was sufficient for me to remind him of the slightest detail on the following day—or even several days thereafter—for him immediately to reproduce, with a pencil or a paintbrush, with astonishing exactitude and in the minutest detail, the plant that had attracted my attention. Furthermore, his eyes, which became fixed, staring directly ahead of him—as if they could pierce the wall to recover the model—had an astonishing faculty of retrospective vision that noticed, recognized and conserved details of tissues or color that had escaped me. If I went to verify for myself whether he might not be the victim of a trick of memory or illusion, I never caught him out in a mistake.

In the same way, whenever I took him to the theater in the town near the château in which his family lived, for a few days afterwards I would catch him standing still, oblivious to everything surrounding him. To my questions, he would reply that he was busy seeing the play once again. If I pressed him, he would describe all the theatrical episodes, in a slow and composed voice, giving them a life that you or I would have qualified as false, but which, I have since understood, was absolutely real to him.

These exceptional faculties only developed further with age. I could say that he lived every day of his life twice, occupying each new day by reliving the previous one—but perhaps it would be more exact to say that he only lived half a life, spending the other half in his memory.

Do I dare to confess everything? In these strange matters one is always afraid, however strong one's conviction and confidence in one's intellect, of appearing to be a liar or a fool. That which surpasses the limits of what we call the possible—as if we could fix its scope!—always seems as vulgar as the product of a sick or imbecilic imagination.

One day—Paul was then 15 years old and his faculty of recapitulation was becoming increasingly obvious—he reminded me about a beggar that we had met, so sordid and sickly that neither Callot nor Goya could ever have desired a model more...realistic. Being very refined, taking delicacy as far as preciousness, he had a horror of those individuals degraded by poverty and drunkenness. This one, to whom he had thrown alms, had caused him a profound disgust, and I can truthfully say that his memory was haunted by it. I perceived that, and attempted to deflect the course of his meditations—but he only replied: "What do you expect? I can see him—he's there!" And he added, grabbing me by the arm—we were in a rather gloomy corner of the park at the time—"It's impossible that you don't see him yourself!"

In truth, for a period of time that was infinitely short—I could not determine the duration of exact fixation—yes, I did see the lame, hairy and hump-backed beggar a few paces away. I definitely saw him appear, full-sized and in color, and disappear instantaneously. Quite unsentimental by nature, and little disposed to admit the inexplicable, I became irritated with myself, attributing my complicity to an almost hypnotic nervous influence that had overcome me, and promised myself not to pay so much attention to morbid illusions in future.

Having no considerable fortune, obliged to create a position for myself, it was inappropriate for me to play games with my brain.

II.

Virginie was an orphan, having lost her father and mother. She had been taken in by her mother's family, an uncle and aunt who brought her up like their own child. That cannot have been an easy task, for she was the most fragile creature imaginable.

Five years younger than Paul, she still seemed a child when he was already well advanced in adolescence. We called her Little Mab, such was her slenderness; her aeriformity—if I may apply such a grandiose word to such a small person—was reminiscent of the Scottish fairy born of a moonbeam.[32]

I remember the first appearance of that amiable doll in Paul's house, where I initially filled the rather thankless role of tutor, but later became a companion and a friend. Have I mentioned that Paul, an orphan himself, lived with a distant female cousin, who, being half paralyzed, retained just enough strength to love and be indulgent?

It was on one of those summer mornings when the sky is veiled by white mist with sharp silver gleams. We were in the garden, immediately in front of the old house, which was decorated by sprays of virginal vines and wisteria. The main gate had been left ajar, following the exit of some tradesman. The invalid was lying on her chaise-longue, smiling, with the expression of amenity

---

[32] The term *aeriformité* is not in the French dictionary, nor is aeriformity in the English one, but *aeriforme* and aeriform (meaning "having the properties of air") exist, thus licensing the coinage in either case.

natural to those who, no longer able to live themselves, take pleasure in watching others live. The lower panel of the gate was slightly elevated.

We had set up a table beside a clump of bushes where the rosy buds of campions were already poking through, and we were studying, with the necessary concentration of mind, one of the most difficult problems of Wronski—that strange scientist of whom Lagrange said that he had reinvented all mathematics and whose proofs had created a new language from scratch, indecipherable to non-initiates.[33] I need to concentrate all my attention in order to conserve my status as master—for with Paul, who was endowed with a marvelous intuition, I was sometimes very fearful of descending to the rank of pupil.

"There's someone behind the gate," Paul told me. He said it in a calm voice, as if he were announcing the simplest thing in the world.

---

[33] Jozef Maria Hoëne (1778-1853), who changed his surname to Wronski, was an ambitious Polish egomaniac who spent the latter part of his life in France and wrote in French because he wanted everyone to have access to the produce of his genius, which was nothing less than a complete reform of philosophy, mathematics and science on neo-Pythagorean lines. The quoted comments by Joseph Lagrange (who really did lay the groundwork for modern mathematical physics) were not intended to be complimentary. Having been universally dismissed as a vain crackpot, Wronski devoted himself arduously, but unfruitfully, to such classic "problems" as squaring the circle, perpetual motion and constructing a machine to predict the future, but he did find one enthusiastic disciple in "Eliphas Lévi," who popularized his reputation as a misunderstood genius in French occult circles. His ironic citation here is subtle testimony to the narrator's unreliability.

I turned my head, and my eyes encountered the lower portion of the gate, solid and wide.

"On the other side?" I said. "One can't see through metal!" But I said no more, for I then perceived that the gate was turning on its hinges, with an exceedingly slow gyration.

Paul was still looking in that direction, and his eyes—with whose nuances I was familiar—had an astonishing fixity. Finally, the new arrival—it was a little girl—revealed herself entirely. When the opening was wide enough for her to slip through, she started running, as if obedient to a violent attraction, and did not stop until she was within a meter of Paul, looking at him with a simultaneously meek and glad expression that made me smile.

Paul's cousin, Mademoiselle de B***, also studied that pretty, pink, blonde apparition, who seemed like a castaway from some Shakespearean fairyland.

It was a little neighbor to whom her aunt had said: "Go and take a look around." She had emerged from the property juxtaposed with Paul's, and then, seeing the gate ajar, had naturally given it a push.

She was about eleven years old. Mademoiselle de B***, perhaps regretting her spinsterhood, was kind to children, and from that day on Virginie had the key to the city in her home, of which she made frequent—or more than frequent—use.

An undeniable sympathy attracted her to Paul; in whatever corner of the park he happened to be—and the garden and wood were vast—she would head straight for him, as if she could perceive him everywhere, and would stop in front of him, smiling daintily.

One day when, to our surprise, the time of her daily visit had long passed, Paul, who was occupied with a most suggestive dissertation on pronunciation of C in pre-Latin languages, made an impatient gesture and exclaimed: "Why hasn't she come? I want her to come!"

A few seconds went by; then I heard a noise of running footsteps, and the child, having cut through the bushes, emerged from a clump of mimosas. She was very pale.

Her uncle came running after her. "But it makes no sense!" he cried. "Can you understand this child, who is ill and whom we were keeping indoors? She escaped from our hands and ran outside. Oh, we knew full well that we'd find her here!"

III.

Between those two creatures—there was no disput-ing it—there existed an intriguing attraction that devel-oped further with every passing day.

Maturity arrived. Paul was then 23, Virginie had reached her 18th year. My pupil had only made modest progress in the practical sciences. Everything that represented current, everyday knowledge was more than indifferent to him, and without his prodigious memory one could have accused him of ignorance on more than one point. On the other hand, he possessed, to an asto-nishing degree, the special faculty that made the Mon-deux and Inaudi veritable prodigies.[34] His persistent memory of shapes and graphic expression of objects in-creased; he seemed to breathe in exterior images in order to transport them into the laboratory of his thoughts and study them at leisure.

In the sympathy that united the two young people, however—and here I can scarcely express the idea that imposes itself upon me—Paul took possession of Virgi-nie; he conquered her and appropriated her. Day by day and minute by minute I had followed that sentiment,

---

[34] Henri Mondeux (1826-1862) and Jacques Inaudi (1867-1950) were the most celebrated of a number of uneducated but seemingly brilliant "calculating prodigies" who attracted en-thusiastic attention in the late 19th century from the likes of Camille Flammarion and Jean-Martin Charcot; they would nowadays be categorized as "high-performing autistic" indi-viduals, whereas Paul would be credited with an eidetic mem-ory.

which was certainly love, in its complete and delightful haunting, but with a very special character. He only lived for her, but she only lived by virtue of him; even if he were absent, she remained impregnated with effluvia with which he had enveloped her. When she was absent, he retained her close to him. I surprised him on several occasions talking to her as if she were by his side, and when I joked about his mistake he would point his finger at empty space, saying: "How can you not see her? She's there!"

Amorous phrases, perhaps—but from the very first, an instinct told me that it was something else, like an evocation, simultaneously internal and external, of the object that filled his thoughts and which, for him alone, was materialized outside of him. I say "for him alone" not daring to affirm anything more.

The worthy Mademoiselle de B*** had followed the progress of that affection, which presented no mysterious character to her, with interest. Paul was rich; his tastes and aptitudes evidently destined him for the placid life of the countryside. Virginie's uncle had died, and her aunt was a valetudinarian. It therefore seemed perfectly natural that Paul should manifest a desire to marry his friend, and, all the proprieties of family and circumstances being in agreement, there was no reason to oppose his desire.

To me, the union had seemed inevitable for a long time. I had understood that Paul would never be equipped to take a role in active life. As a dreamer, everything in him derived from the interior sanctuary. The most stupid of city-bred laborers would have got the better of his inexperience. As for Virginie, she no longer belonged to herself. As their intimacy became tighter, she was, so to speak, annihilated in him, initially of her own accord, and also—perhaps especially—by reason of the dominion he exercised over her moral being, which was an anticipated possession more absolute than that of marriage. Between the two of them there was a flux and reflux of vitality; it was not so much that they belonged to one another as that they absorbed one another.

The marriage, a veritable consecration, in the purest and most elevated sense of the term, took place.

As long as I live I shall never forget that luminous and radiant nuptial ceremony, which made them—as I then believed—companions in delight and distress forever: united in joy and in sorrow, as the Calvinist liturgy has it.

In the sheaf on sunbeams falling from the stained-glass windows, I had a momentary illusion that the two beings, by virtue of an effect of synchrony, were blended into one. There was, at that moment, an equilibrium between the two creatures who were giving themselves to one another with a mutual abnegation of the self.

On the very morning of the ceremony I had accepted a mission to the Orient, with an obligation to leave immediately. Having been a witness to their nascent happiness, I was glad not to hinder its blossoming in any way with my presence. As we left the church I made my farewells. Shaking their hands, which were clasped together in mine, I could not tell which was which.

I gave them one last farewell wave, convinced that practical life would sooner or later take possession of my two heroes of fairyland—who, entered into the norms of social banality, would grow old as good prosaically-enlightened spouses.

A letter that reached me in Hong Kong shook my conviction; they had buried themselves in the depths of the Sologne, where, it appeared, they were living completely alone, happy not to hear any echo of real life. I replied with good wishes that were certainly quite sincere.

A year later, in Laos, I received a letter from Paul, striking in its strangeness. Bizarre as it is, it ought to form part of this manuscript, which is a sort of case-study, so I shall transcribe it in its entirety.

IV.

My friend, do you remember the interesting study that you had me undertake one day of the second chapter of *Genesis*, when, thanks to the luminous restitutions of that linguistic visionary Fabre d'Olivet,[35] we followed the mysterious work of creative nature step by step, seeking the fact beneath the symbol, the material meaning beneath the esoteric enigma? Having reached the sublime verse that manifests, in a few words, the creation of woman—of Aischa,[36] of Eve—we stopped, hesitant before the intimate and profound suggestion that solicited us to reconstitute that scene, the beauty of which surpasses the most enthusiastic dreams of the imagination.

---

[35] Antoine Fabre d'Olivet (1767-1825) was a neo-Pythagorean philosopher who produced, among other books, a study of *La Langue hébraïque restituée* (1816-16; tr. as *The Hebrew Language Restored*), which used presumed equivalences between Hebrew letters and Egyptian hieroglyphics to "decipher" various texts, most importantly *Genesis*, and to reveal supposed hidden meanings therein. Although the discovery of the Rosetta Stone, which allowed Egyptian hieroglyphs to be properly decoded, devastated his theories, he retained (and still retains) a certain following among occultists, especially Kabbalists.

[36] Aischa, also rendered Aisha or Ayesha, is an Arabic name allegedly meaning "She Who Lives;" Fabre d'Olivet credits it to "the woman" derived from Adam's rib in *Genesis* 2—who is distinguished from Eve in some decodings—but it is nowadays more familiar as the name of Mohammed's favorite wife and H. Rider Haggard's favorite anti-heroine, *She*.

We passed on—but I had retained in my ear, like an echo that was never to be extinguished, the radiant canticle of Adam Kadmon crying: "Wa-iaômer ha-Adam Zoâth…" or "This is now bones of my bones and flesh of my flesh."[37]

The name Aischa, the veritable formula of the Will of which the woman was the Realization haunted me like the enunciation of a problem whose solution was always withheld.

Now, that solution—with what glory—I have found! You alone, perhaps, can understand me, because your intellect moves on a superior plane of Intuition. To me, nothing seems more evident and clear.

See for yourself:

In the human, the concrete representation of collective humanity, all aspirations existed in a latent state, and in order to be manifest, only awaited a volitional effort—a shove from inside to outside, so to speak.

The Human Adam, then both male and female, enjoyed external nature egotistically, blossoming in the glare of it splendors—and the more he admired beauty, the greater his thirst for beauty became. But that supreme Beauty to which he aspired, he could not see, be-

---

[37] I have rendered the translation of this quotation (from *Genesis* 2:24) in the form given to it in the Authorized Version. The Hebrew version quoted first is taken directly from Fabre d'Olivet, and exemplifies his eccentric orthography. In neo-Pythagorean and Kabbalistic mysticism, Adam Kadmon, the Primal Man, is a kind of archetype, in the image of which the Earthly or Human Adam was created; the archetype's form is replicated in that of the entire universe—the Great Man—as well as mere human beings, according to the principle of "As Above, So Below."

cause it was within him, in his dual, as-yet-unseparated nature

Can you understand that torture: to feel in oneself beauty, Love, to possess the notion of it, the intimate sensation of it, and not be able to contemplate it face to face, nor embrace it. Think what a miser might experience who had a gold ingot for a heart, without being able to rip open his breast in order to possess it!

In vain the vibrant immensities expanded around Adam, in vain the Nebulae pregnant with star-worlds threw forth dust. What was all that compared with what he desired: the Companion, the Supreme Beauty, who—this is the text itself—was to emanate from him, only then presenting to him the reflection of his intimate sensation?

And it was in one of these crises of sublime and torturous Desire that the miracle was accomplished of the Exteriorization of Beauty and Love—which were within him and which sprang forth from him, in the Ideal Form, Grace and Harmony condensed in the Being who was truly the flesh of his flesh, the formally radiant Essence of triumphant Humanity: Woman!

And Adam Kadmon knelt before Her, grateful for the exquisite suffering of the extraction, and stammered the first Hosannah of love!

Having a scientific mind, I am never pleased by these shrill reveries of an overexcited imagination. In guiding Paul in his Hebraic studies, my sole purpose had been to give him a clear and non-routine notion of the science of roots, and nothing more. Although Fabre d'Olivet interests me as a linguist, I had always wished—and still do—to stop short of his Theosophico-Buddhist hypotheses. Thus, I experienced a real chagrin in observing that my pupil was not only infatuated with such chimeras, but was exaggerating them to excess.

I sent a few words to that effect in reply, insisting on the dangers that might be run by reason of those fantasies, whose least fault is to deflect the mind away from more practical preoccupations. I was still counting on marriage and paternity to give his moral activity more substantial nourishment.

When I had sent my letter, I had a few pangs of remorse, dreading, because of Paul's slightly unhealthy susceptibility, that I had given my advice an overly ironic tone. After all, was I not pursuing my own chimera in my research on prehistoric peoples, identifying the Cimmerians of Herodotus with the ancient Khmers of Cambodia? Hypothesis is the great seductress, and whoever has not followed her crazy track is ignorant of the greatest human joys.

Finally, after three years of absence, I decided to return to France, with a wealth of notes and documents in support of my favorite theses.

On arriving back in our colonial ports, I experienced a veritable discomfort at not finding a letter from

Paul. Had I, then, wounded him with a little inoffensive mockery? I would have been sorry for that, and I promised myself firmly that, once I had disembarked, I would explain myself and extract an amicable pardon from him—with multiple *mea culpa*s, if necessary.

I took just enough time to take care of some necessary business in Paris; then, without warning the person that I expected to surprise in full happiness, I installed myself in a railway carriage bound for Vierzon. I stopped, in accordance with the directions Paul had given me in one of his earliest letters, at the station of Salbris, a large town whose name is linked to one of the most honorable episodes of the war of 1870.[38]

I hastened to go into the local inn to order a frugal meal. The end of October was approaching, and the shortening of the days advised me to arrive as soon as possible at the Château de Pierre-Sèche,[39] where my friends lived. I still had five hours before me. I made enquiries about a carriage, which was procured for me with the best will in the world.

"Where is Monsieur going?" asked the innkeeper.

---

[38] When Leon Gambetta took charge of the French forces, on behalf of the Government of National Defense, after the fall of Napoléon III, he gathered 60,000 of the hastily-drafted makeshift troops of the 15th and 16th divisions at Salbris, in Loiret-Cher. The Prussians, whose intelligence was faulty, did not realize that the town had been reinforced and attacked it with too few troops, suffering one of the few setbacks of their relentless descent. Lermina was there, and must have been well aware of his good fortune in being able to take part in one of the very few battles in which the French, ill-trained and ill-equipped as they were, actually had the upper hand.

[39] Appoximately "Dry-Stone Castle"

I named the aforementioned château. The man assumed a contrite expression. "It's more than four leagues away, in the middle of a marsh, on the left bank of the Sauldre," he told me.

I had noticed the change in his physiognomy; I did not imagine that it was the distance or the poor quality of the terrain that had provoked it. Prey to a vague anxiety, I continued: "You know the owners, no doubt?"

This time his embarrassment was undeniable. "Does Monsieur mean Monsieur Paul X?"

"Indeed—I'm a friend of his. I've just got back from a long voyage, and am eager to shake his hand."

"Monsieur is just back from a long voyage? Perhaps, then, he does not know…"

"What?"

"That Monsieur Paul never receives anyone, and that no one can boast of seeing him for more than six months. Oh, it's a great pity, Monsieur, a veritable pity!"

"What do you mean? Has he suffered some misfortune?"

"When I said that Monsieur did not know…the poor little lady is dead."

"Dead!" I cried, in profound anguish. "What! You mean Paul's wife, that dear and exquisite creature?"

"Monsieur is absolutely right; it has been a great loss to the region. Believe me or not, Monsieur, but everyone loved her, and wept for her too, for she was a long time dying. She was so weak! The château is badly situated, you see, and people catch fever there. I don't understand why Monsieur Paul brought a delicate woman like that to it."

So it really was her that had died! I had never felt a blow so dolorous. Its brutality had literally choked me, and tears were falling from my eyes.

"I can see that Monsieur is a friend," the landlord went on. "Perhaps I ought not have told him about it so bluntly, but Monsieur would have found out soon enough. Is it still necessary to order the carriage?"

"Certainly!" I cried. "Why not? Should we abandon our friends when they are in pain? Oh, I wish to God that I had come back sooner. I might have been able to prevent this horrid misfortune!"

"It's doubtful, Monsieur, for the little lady was very ill. I must also say that Monsieur Paul looked after her! Oh, it was beautiful and tragic at the same time. He never left her, and when they went out, with him supporting her, I swear that you would have thought that he was drinking her in with his eyes! He loved her a great deal, that's obvious! So his despair is understandable. Since the day when the poor lady was taken to be buried, with all the neighborhood behind her—and tears as true as yours just now—Monsieur Paul has shut himself away in his home, and has never—never, you hear—never left Pierre-Sèche since.

The details were heart-rending. Paul was living alone in that château—which, it was said, would be his tomb, as it had been that of his dear wife. He had no one with him but an old domestic, who was also—to use the innkeeper's expression—"Spinning a bad thread".

And then...there was something else.

It was difficult to persuade my informant to explain more clearly—in fact, it was just as difficult for him to do so. Naturally, everywhere death passes, it leaves a wake of fear. In this case, strange rumors had spread through the region; there was talk of fantastic lights appearing by night in the windows of the château. A woman who had been hired to provide domestic services had refused to return, declaring that she would never go back into a house haunted by ghosts.

Oh, the innkeeper did not believe a word of this foolishness—but how could one stop people taking? Anyway, was it not bizarre that a man of Paul's age should shut himself away like that? He had refused absolutely to see anyone, even well-intentioned people who wanted to bring him consolation. The door remained pitilessly closed to them. Old Jean—that was the name of the domestic, whom I knew well—hustled people away distractedly. One might easily think that he had gone mad too!

"All in all, Monsieur," the worthy fellow continued, "if you want to get into that house of misfortune, I think you'll have difficulty doing so."

"I shall try, just the same," I replied.

Deep down, I did not doubt that I would be let in. Knowing Paul's exquisite delicacy, I was not unduly astonished by a claustration that was adequately explained by such justified despair. I would see him, I would talk to him, and I would succeed in galvanizing his numbed soul, revivifying his dead heart. That was my duty as a friend, and I would not shirk it.

VI.

You will remember the glacial prose of Edgar Poe: *"and at length found myself, as the shades of the evening drew on, within view of the melancholy House of Usher. I know not how it was—but, with the first glimpse of the building, a sense of insufferable gloom pervaded my spirit."*[40]

That reminiscence—the House of Usher—obsessed me all along the route as, huddled in the carriage driven by a silent Solognot jaundiced by ancient fevers, I followed the road along the edge of a marsh on the left bank of the Sauldre that led to Pierre-Sèche, beneath the heavy grey sky of that autumnal evening.

My driver was not one of those men that one interrogates in quest of anecdotes. He was one of those non-thinkers repelled by any intellectual expansion. He went straight ahead, looking neither to one side nor the other, ruminating something with his heavy prognathous jaws.

That society did not displease me at all, leaving intact a reverie that gradually condensed in somnolence. I had not closed my eyes, however; between my half-closed eyelids the dull, grey heath went by, in which the steely reflection of a pond sometimes glinted, like a blade of light. The wheels moved soundlessly on the hard road, while the macabre shadow of the horse was stretched out.

---

[40] I have, of course, substituted the original text from Poe's "The Fall of the House of Usher," where Lermina cites Charles Baudelaire's translation.

I could not say that the route seemed long to me, for I no longer had any notion of time, nor any clear comprehension of objects. I was caught within the vice of an anguish that I could not analyze but gripped me so tightly that I was stifled. And on the flat, empty plain, between the pools—blackish scabs on a dirty brown skin—I went forward incessantly, without knowing where, instinctively anxious.

It was while the remembrance of the House of Usher was imposing itself most despotically that, while facing a sheet of water several meters wide and the entrance of a wooden bridge closed by a gate, the man turned round and spoke for the first time, saying: "Pierre-Sèche."

I awoke with a start. I almost asked him what Pierre-Sèche had to do with me—but I was seized by an impression very different from what I had expected.

On the other side of the pool, in which long grasses were asleep, nodding their heads like ripe wheat, on the summit of a low hillock that seemed composed of decorative stonework and mosaics, stood a sort of castle, one wing of which projected in front of me, boldly silhouetted against a sky reddened by the setting sun.

For the vision of the dead House of Usher, which had appeared to me in my desolate previsions like the face of a hypochrondriac, was substituted a dashing profile with a certain refined elegance. Red-tufted wild vines ran along the walls, their supportive skeleton provided by ribs of ivy clinging to the flint, a purple embroidery on green velvet. Its form was enveloped by a light, iridescent mist, which blurred its contours and attenuated its angles.

In my state of mind, that scene, simultaneously unexpected and charming, delighted me.

Meanwhile, the man sat still, waiting for me to decide to get down. I understood that, his job being done, he was astonished that I was not setting him free; he was oblivious to the fantasies of my imagination. I leapt to the ground and handed him a coin.

"Is this really the Château de Pierre-Sèche?" I asked him.

"As I told you…"

"Thank you. You may return to Salbris."

He looked at me with his colorless eyes; I thought that he was not satisfied.

"Isn't the price right?" I asked.

"Yes—but there's the gate. There's a bell."

Good! He considered that his duty was not to abandon me until I had gone in. Given my vague presentiment of strange events, however, I did not want him to witness a possible disappointment.

"Go," I said to him. "Don't worry about me."

He made up his mind then, turned the horse around, drew away and disappeared.

I remained alone in front of the metal gate. It barred the entire width of the little bridge I mentioned, whose balustrade-less decking could not be reached from outside. Beneath it was the pool, mossy and motionless. Beyond the bridge, a pathway climbed up the hillock, then disappeared around a corner.

The windows facing the pool—I counted three—were closed. The shadows of vines and ivy blackened the panes; one might that imagined them as three black eyes veiled by lashes. I felt as if they were looking at me—but if someone inside had observed my presence, why had he not presented himself at the gate?

I told myself then that I was thinking crazily, and that, in truth, I was creating an impression of mystery at my leisure, since there was a bell and a chain.

I shook the chain.

VII.

I saw the bell rise and fall; it was quite a large one, and for a moment I feared that I might have sounded it too loudly—but it did not ring. I tried again, with the same result. The clapper had been removed.

That annoyed me, for the hypothesis presented itself to my mind for the first time that I might find myself stupidly stopped at this door, with darkness falling, having failed to bring my journey to a conclusion, effectively lost in a region that I did not know.

I would not admit that I was beaten, though. I drew away a little, trying to catch sight of something in the château or the little park. There was no sign of life or movement. I went along the side of the pool, thinking that I might go around it and reach Pierre-Sèche from some other direction, but I soon perceived that it surrounded the property on all sides.

The craggy eminence on which the castle was constructed formed a veritable island. Moreover, the terrain was marshy to the point that I risked getting bogged down in the mud at every step.

It is necessary to admit that my situation was rather strange—not to say ridiculous. I was in the middle of France, at a friend's door, a hundred times more embarrassed that I would have been in a barbaric land. The worst thing was that the cerebral tension from which I was suffering was injurious to my mental lucidity, and I was having great difficulty thinking what to do, although it hardly required much imagination.

The bell had no clapper, but it was there. Moreover, it was fixed to the gatepost itself—inside, to be sure, but not out of reach. I hoisted myself up on the bars with one hand and, brandishing my cane in the other, I landed a vigorous blow on the metal. This time, I had the desired effect; the sound vibrated quite clearly, and my belated ingenuity was crowned with success.

Scarcely two minutes had elapsed when I saw someone appear at the far end of the path that came down the hillock—but that individual, doubtless suspicious, appeared to place his hands above his eyes in order to examine the intruder, and then made extravagant significant gestures instructing him to go away.

This was awkward. I understood that, if the man disappeared, it would be futile for me to summon him again—but remembering that, according to the innkeeper, the only inhabitant of the house save for my old friend was the old servant that I had once known very well, I shouted as loudly as I could: "Jean! Hey, Jean, it's me!" And, in case the "it's me" was insufficiently suggestive, I called out my name with the full force of my lungs.

Victory! I was not mistaken. The man raced down rapidly, reached the little bridge, arrived at the gate and said: "You! It's really you! Oh, what luck! My God— why didn't you come sooner!"

"Sooner or later," I replied, "here I am. Open the door, old chap, and, if I can be of any service here, you know that you can count on me."

Jean was an old man, almost 70 years old, thin and bent. He made hand-signals asking me to moderate the sound of my voice.

"Listen," he said. "I'm under absolutely strict orders never to let anyone in—but you, that's something else, and I'll take it on myself to violate the instruction. Just promise that you'll do as I say...yes, yes, I said do as I say. Death has been here, and I'm not sure that it won't call again..."

The old man's tone was replete with profound emotion. I did my best to give him confidence; the gate opened, and I went in.

"Before anything else, you see," he continued, "I need to talk to you. You're wiser than me; perhaps you'll understand. Personally, I've been afraid that my poor master's mind has been unhinged..." At the foot of the château he paused. "Not that way," he said, brusquely. "He mustn't see you. Follow me—we'll be all right in a moment."

He took the greatest precautions not to make any noise, and I did likewise. We reached a little side-door, the only opening in the western façade, and went into a sort of pantry—or, rather, a fruit-store. The night was almost completely dark.

"Sit down," said Jean. "I beg your pardon for receiving you like this, but it's necessary." Shaking his head, he repeated: "It's necessary. I'm going to see that everything's in order...and make sure that he doesn't suspect anything."

I was impatient; after all, I knew my friend Paul well enough to have no fear of seeing him again. If that were to provoke a crisis of despair, I would take the necessary control of him, and that very explosion, too long contained, would be salutary.

Jean soon came back.

"Monsieur hasn't noticed anything. He's in his study, as he always is at this hour, and will be until tomorrow morning. We're alone—quite alone—so we can talk. Mind you, I'm wondering now whether you did well in coming."

"There'll be time to determine whether I was right or wrong," I replied, rather sharply, "when I've heard you out. For now, I can assure you that I will be able to free Paul from this abominable sadness."

We were sitting in the dark, and I could scarcely make out old Jean's features. I saw him stiffen in a start of surprise, though. "Sadness?" he said. "Who told you that Monsieur Paul is sad?"

"Isn't that natural after the frightful misfortune that has struck him?"

"Oh yes! And yet no—that's not it. You're on the wrong track, entirely. Wait while I light the lamp. I'm no coward, having been a soldier, but here I don't like to remain in darkness."

I was beginning to wonder whether the old man was in his right mind himself, and whether, in talking to me about his master's unhinged mind, he was not attributing his own mental weakness to Paul.

When the lamp was lit, I looked at him. He was quite robust. His once-coarse features had been refined by a patina of age; his eyes were clear, his gaze direct.

"Come on, old chap," I said to him, heartily, "you and I aren't children; we know what human grief is and how it can disturb the most well-adjusted souls. You're leading a solitary life here, which isn't conducive to clarity of thought. I've arrived with a fresh mind and a well-equilibrated intellect. Tell me what has happened, and I'll give you my opinion."

Jean sat down facing me, unceremoniously, with his hands on his knees. "Yes, Monsieur, I know you for a man of good sense, and a good heart too—otherwise, I wouldn't have let you in. But there are things here of which you have no idea, and won't be easy for you to believe—it wouldn't astonish me much if you were to leave without having tried."

"Let's get on with it, then. Paul's alive—that's the main thing. If he's ill, we'll cure him; if he's mad…"

"Don't bother with suppositions; let me tell you everything. Don't interrupt me—I've had enough trouble already, getting my head around all of this."

The best way to get through it was to let him tell it in his own way. I kept quiet.

He told me nothing about the earliest phase of the marriage that surprised me. Virginie adored her husband, in the sane and profound sense of the word. He returned that affection, with an emphatic element of loving domination, which was also absorbing. The two creatures were the entire world to one another. Their understanding was so perfect, the adaptation of their two natures so complete that, to tell the truth—these were Jean's words—the two of them were a single person. Their mental intimacy rendered the use of words almost unnecessary. They could be seen contemplating one another for hours on end without saying a word.

"One might have thought that they weren't talking," Jean went on, "but I'm sure that they were; they heard one another internally. Often, Madame would give me an order that came from Monsieur, I was sure—even though he hadn't said anything, she heard him thinking."

What emerged from these observations, subtler than one might have expected from an uneducated man, was that Virginie had abdicated all will-power and initiative. Love had produced the phenomenon that her individuality had melted into Paul's.

"What I'm telling you must see odd, but it seems to me that she didn't even take the trouble to think any longer; her voice was no more than a breath, as if she had no need to speak. More than that, I'd say that she was disappearing physically—yes, when I looked at her, I got the idea that she was fading away, like those photographs that one leaves in the sun, and which become indistinct."

In brief, beneath Maître Jean's slightly wordy circumlocutions, it was evident that poor Virginie had taken ill with some wasting disease: anemia, consumption—I couldn't be sure. It seemed to me that the good servant, by virtue of the fervent loyalty he had to his employers, had seen them in a somewhat fantastic light. It was merely a matter of dolorous but perfectly natural facts; perhaps her passion for Paul had not been adequate to sustain the poor girl's strength.

The certain thing was that she had died, and I became involuntarily irritated by the old man's prolixity, complicating incidents that were easily explicable.

"All in all," I said, with ill-contained impatience, "poor Virginie continued to decline, and Paul had the pain of losing her. I don't doubt the intensity of his despair…"

"For the first month, Monsieur, it was as if he were overwhelmed. He spent days lying down, not moving, with his eyes shut, as pale as the corpse that had been taken away…"

"And that state has been complicated by an ever-increasing prostration, with the result that today…"

"But no, not at all!" cried Jean, trying to impose silence on me with extravagant gestures. "Monsieur isn't letting me speak—evidently he thinks that I want to impose on him. You assume that Monsieur Paul is sad, in despair, and that's the reason why he doesn't want to see anyone. You're completely mistaken. Monsieur Paul isn't sad, and he isn't ill—it's something else entirely…"

"Explain yourself, then!"

"One morning, about a month after Madame's death, when I went into Monsieur's bedroom, I was very surprised to find that he wasn't in bed. The most astonishing thing of all was that he was smiling, for the first time in many days. He ate a great deal, with an appetite I no longer recognized, and even drank—too much, in my opinion. Then, after the meal, he fell into a sleep so profound, and so rapid, that I left him stretched out on the sofa and retired discreetly. I went up several times during the day to make sure that he didn't need anything; he slept like that until the evening. Finally, he woke up, and I advised him to go to bed. I was convinced that dejection had broken him, to the point of requiring him to rest for 24 hours—but he replied quite sharply that I could spare him my advice. All that he wanted from me was not to come up to his apartment for any reason, unless I was summoned. I took him at his word and, since that day. I've never been into my master's room between 6 p.m. and 10 a.m."

"What does he do during that time?"

"How do I know? His life is still regulated as follows: at ten 10 a.m., he rings and I got to his room; he's standing up, still smiling, with a happy expression that has something supernatural about it...yes, almost frightening. His study is always locked, and I haven't been into it for five months. After breakfast, he lies down on the sofa and goes to sleep. At about 5 p.m., he rings again and gives me a few instructions. I go away...and that's all!"

This was, indeed, beginning to appear singular, presenting the symptoms of a mental derangement.

"You say that Paul seems happy, joyful...and never sees anyone..."

"Oh, I can answer for that. In the morning, I watch out for the tradesmen, and I wait for them at the gate, so that they won't ring. I've removed the clapper, and I'll remove the bell itself..."

"In sum," I went on, confidently, "it seems to me that there's an amelioration in his state of health. He's drinking, and sleeping. I don't see any more than this obsessive claustration and this inversion of normal habits, which makes him sleep by day and stay awake at night. What's his physical condition? Is he weak or strong, vigorous or anemic?"

"There's something about him that frightens me— it's his pallor—and yet...should I confess everything?" Jean lowered his voice. "I think...yes, I really think that he..." And without pronouncing the word, he raised his thumb above his lips.

"That would be more frightful than all the rest!" I exclaimed. "But you know perfectly well, I suppose, whether he asks you for brandy, for absinthe..."

"No, it's not that. He only gets me to bring one kind of liquor, with which I'm not familiar, with such a strong taste and odor...hang on; I've got a bottle here that I'll take up to him tomorrow morning..."

The bottle was sealed with a glass stopper, but the characteristic odor struck me immediately: it was ether. I shivered; in the Far East I had encountered ether-drinkers, and drunkenness had never seemed to me to be so murderous. It was worse than poisoning; it was a slow, irresistible combustion, corroding all the organs...

"But if that's true, you must have noticed his nervous tremors. His breath must be impregnated with that odor."

"No, I haven't noticed that. What's more, his room doesn't reek of that odor—I'd certainly recognize it through his study door."

That threw me slightly. "Good!" I said, again. "One can be cured of any evil passion. I understand your anxieties, my friend, but I hope to be able to set them at rest before long. I shall see your master; you shall announce my arrival with such precautions as you may deem necessary. Don't worry—I shall be able to make good excuses for your disobedience. I shall resume an influence over him that my amity and cool head will ensure. Don't wait another minute. Go up, my dear Jean— I'll wait for you here."

Far from obeying me, though, Jean shook his head.

"Why hesitate? You can't doubt Paul's affection for me. All right, he doesn't see anyone—but it's me!"

Jean stood up and walked around the room, prey to a visible embarrassment. As I watched him curiously, wondering what had got into him now, he suddenly stopped in front of me and fixed his wide-open eyes upon me.

"Not tonight, Monsieur, not tonight. I'll try tomorrow morning at ten o'clock, but not tonight!"

"Why not?"

"Because...." He seemed to gather all his courage. "Because at night...he isn't alone!"

"What?" I said, leaping out of my chair.

"Ah! There it is! Now you're asking yourself whether old Jean is mad, fit for a straitjacket. Come on, do you really think that that I haven't tried to make sense of it? I'm a man...and a servant...." He laughed dryly. "Do you think that I don't spy on my master?"

"A very honorable espionage, since it has no purpose other than his own good. But after all, in order for him not to be…alone, it would be necessary for someone to be introduced into the château, and you affirm…"

Then, leaning toward me, Jean told me things so bizarre that I listened to them as if in a nightmare—and those things were such that I decided not to make any attempt to see Paul that night.

It was agreed that I would be announced the following morning, at 10 a.m.

VIII.

It was with a veritable anxiety that I waited for Jean the following day while, as he had promised, he went to notify his master of my presence.

I had slept little, and badly—which would have been sufficiently explained by my preoccupations, if I had not been prey to sensations of a very particular sort. In the course of the night, I had been subject to a sort of suffocation, as if I had suddenly been deprived of air—or, rather, that the air had changed its nature and was no longer suited to the action of my lungs.

Something was happening around me that was incomprehensible, and also invisible. Dare I say what I thought? It was like an impression of the other world, a slippage on a plane that was no longer that of the living. I had neither the energy nor even the desire to resist, complacently accepting the depression, which was limited to feeling faint, with an ineffable joy of abandonment.

However, reason coming to my aid, I wondered whether there might not be some bouquet to flowers in my room that was making me dizzy. I searched, and found none. Eventually, I fell into a prostration that no longer allowed anything to subsist in my brain but vague nightmares in which I was surrounded by dilute vapors, formed into cloudy sketches of beings.

Fortunately daylight had dissipated all such anguish.

"Victory!" said Jean, as he entered my room. "It went a thousand times better than I hoped. Monsieur Paul is waiting for you."

"So much the better. Just one word, old chap—how is he this morning?"

"As he always is: smiling, happy. If only he didn't have that accursed pallor! One might think that there's no longer a drop of blood in his veins."

"We'll see to that. Trust me, my good man—and lead me to him."

"You don't have far to go, for you're in the bedroom directly above his study. A few steps to go down, and that's all."

We went. I had one last fit of embarrassment, wondering what expression I ought to adopt, but I did not have time to think about it; a door had opened, and Pail was coming toward me, with his hands extended.

He was indeed very pale, as if drained of blood; his general appearance, however, was not disquieting. The strong grip of his fingers convinced me that the man was vigorous.

I had not dared to say a single word, fearing to make a false step; I simply looked at him, with my full attention.

"Yes, yes, look at me, my friend," he said. "Look hard at the man who is before you, and has nothing more to desire now that you have come."

That welcome surpassed all my hopes; I was perfectly content with it.

"Right," he said. "We'll have breakfast, and then, with glasses in hand, we'll chat with open hearts. Are you still a connoisseur of wines? I have a certain *cru* here of which I'd like your opinion. Ha, ha! My dear friend, you wouldn't believe how radiantly joyful I feel! It's so good to be away from the world, away from everything, with those one loves!"

Needless to say, that attitude troubled me. While fearful of a crisis of grief, I had not imagined that it could be avoided, when scarcely six months had elapsed since poor Virginie's death. I experienced disappointment, and also a vague anger directed against such a prompt moral revival.

For a moment, I had an idea that he might be playing a part to reassure my friendship, but I could not sustain it, so natural did his effusions seem. He had drawn me to a sofa to sit beside him, and while Jean—seemingly-impassive, but actually very intrigued by what was happening—laid the table next to a large leaded window.

Paul interrogated me as to what I had been doing since our separation, taking an interest in my work and my achievements. I replied as best I could, trying to shake off the anxiety that was weighing upon me, disturbing the clarity of my mind.

"Bah!" he said. "Good wine will loosen your tongue—for, in truth, you don't seem to be your usual self. You aren't ill, are you?"

It was almost comic—he was the one who was now inquiring about my health!

Jean sometimes questioned me with his gaze, surreptitiously. If he had interrogated me out loud, I would have found it very difficult to answer him, so troubled did I feel, quite unable to formulate any appreciation at all.

Paul seemed to be quite free of care, and when we were sitting at the table, facing one another, no one would ever have imagined that there was any subject of grief between us. He urged me to talk about myself; I thought that he was cleverly trying to avoid any conversation about himself.

He ate heartily—intelligently, I ought to add—like a man determined to maintain his health and recover his strength. He was drinking a wine that was slightly inebriating but generative of energy.

I shall not astonish anyone by saying that I was thinking continually about a means of bringing up the one question that was burning my lips. I tried hard to work out the cause of an insensitivity that I persisted in thinking apparent. But why the dissimulation? Was he experiencing some stupid shame at the prospect of letting his true feelings show through in front of his servant? Was he putting on the stoicism for my benefit?

When the coffee was served, he addressed a significant signal to Jean. He wanted to be left alone with me. Jean winked in my direction; like me he assumed that the moment for frankness and confidences had arrived.

Paul stretched himself out in his armchair and said:

"Ah! My dear chap, it's good to be alive! Come on, sincerely, how do you find me? In good condition, no? For myself, I've never felt as solid. Look at me, and give me your honest opinion."

I have said that apart from his extraordinary pallor, he presented all the characteristics of health. I was thus able to reply in all honesty as he desired me to do. However, taking the bull by the horns, as they say, I could not help adding: "I'm all the more happy to find you thus because I feared something else entirely, after the frightful misfortune that has struck you."

As I pronounced that sentence, which summed up all my preoccupations, I looked him full in the face. At that moment he pushed away his coffee and grasped a liqueur bottle in his free hand. He was not tremulous; there was not the slightest nervous quiver.

"Yes, yes, I know," he said, smiling. "Given your friendship, the contrary would have astonished me—but you can see that I'm standing up to the situation quite robustly…"

He was definitely mad! That lightness of tone, almost ironic, was revolting! Poor girl! How could you have been so promptly, so abominably forgotten!

He had poured out the chartreuse and was swallowing it in little sips.

I suppressed a gesture of indignation, with great difficulty. I contented myself with saying, dryly: "Well, bully for you! I confess that I had dreaded that the death of your wife might have dealt you a terrible blow, but I can see that my friendship has no need to expend itself in consolations…"

His face radiant, he said: "No—there's no need for that!"

I almost knocked the table over with an angry gesture. "Accept me excuses, then. I observed that great changes have overtaken you, for there was a time when poor Virginie occupied a far greater place in your soul." Powerless to feign self-composure any longer, I cried: "In fact, you adored her! You adored her as she herself adored you. But the poor girl is dead, and after six months I find you with a smile on your lips and dry eyes! Pardon me for being surprised. I don't doubt that you have excellent reasons for standing up so robustly— according to your own expression—to a grief of which others, doubtless less well-endowed, might have died. If you would deign to let me know what they are, at least you will permit me to reserve my appreciation in all liberty…"

I had let all that out in a single breath, impatient to empty my heart, clearly risking a rupture.

Very calmly, with his eternal smile, he had not interrupted me. When I shut up, he shrugged his shoulders slightly. "Then you too," he said, simply, "believe that Virginie is dead?"

I shuddered in my chair, while a cold sweat emerged on my temples. The evidence was compelling. Madness! The poor fellow had lost his mind...and everything became clear, in a sinister light. Oh, how unjust I had been!

The blow had been so violent that, unable to master myself immediately, I stammered: "Yes...I thought...I was told!"

"I won't hold your outburst against you, then. If the people who had informed you had told the truth, I would be guilty of a great offense, and would merit the reproaches that your friendship has attenuated too much. Virginie dead! At the mere thought of it...look! My eyes are filling with tears."

"Then...I've been deceived, and Virginie is alive! I beg you, Paul, not to play games with me. I love you truly, sincerely—your joy and grief are mine. After all, it's possible...but how can what those people told me be explained? They said they had been present at the funeral ceremony, had followed the poor child to the cemetery, and unless one supposes that they have all been victims of a hallucination, I couldn't doubt..."

As I raised my voice, Paul made a gesture bidding me to calm down. "They're not mad, or malevolent. They're talking about appearances; their good faith isn't in question. What they told you about the burial and the cemetery is quite true."

I passed my hands over my forehead. I had surely gone astray in a nightmare; I needed to get back to reality, to logic. "Will you answer my questions clearly?" I asked him.

"Willingly. Ask them."

"During these obsequies to which the entire region bore witness, was the coffin empty?"

"No."

"Between the wooden planks, was it or was it not the body of Virginie that was laid to eternal rest?"

"It was her body."

"Was the inhumation completed, to the end?"

"To the end?"

"Listen, Paul. I think I understand, and yet I hesitate to question you further. Have you, with frightful courage, some night, in your loneliness, raised a sacrilegious hand over that scarcely-sealed tomb and removed its sacred deposit? And then, as has been known before, having found the unfortunate woman alive, have you carried her off in your arms? Then, in an unimaginable terror for which no one can blame you, have you hidden her, sequestered her here?"

And I looked around, seized by a quasi-superstitious dread.

He laughed. "Well, here you are losing yourself in the middle of a romance. That's straight out of a feuilleton melodrama. Are we children, to get caught up in such nonsense?"

"But in the end, dead or alive, there's no intermediate..."

Suddenly, he became very serious. "That's what they say," he whispered, "intoxicated with words, posing axioms with an audacity that is only equaled by their carelessness. Dead or alive! That *or* is marvelous!"

He fell silent, as if fearful that he had said too much, but I did not intend that he should stop in midstream. For me the thing was indubitable: in that brain, apparently quite sane, there was what I irreverently called a crack.

"Why does that *or* seem so strange to you?"

He looked me full in the face. "Because it implies antagonism," he replied, curtly. "Because it signifies an incompatibility between the two states."

"Dare you claim that one can be dead and alive at the same time?"

Between his last reply and mine, something had happened, with a rapidity that was almost disturbing. The light in Paul's eyes had suddenly become veiled, almost extinct, and his eyelids, having abruptly become heavy, had half-closed over the orbs.

"What's the matter with you?" I exclaimed. "One would think you were falling asleep!"

He made a violent and obvious effort to open his eyes. "Yes, yes," he murmured. "That's it. I can't think any more. I need...to sleep! I can't resist, and I don't think I have the right...yes, it would be a crime!" He was speaking in a dull, toneless voice, as if in a dream.

Frightened, I got up and went to him.

"Don't be afraid," he continued, "and above all, don't question me. I don't know yet if I can tell you everything. I have to ask, to consult. You're staying here, aren't you? The house is yours—I only reserve this apartment for myself. I have to sleep...to sleep...and then...."

His head slumped on to his breast. It was a brutal collapse.

"I'm at your disposal," I told him. "I shall watch over you."

He shuddered. "No, I don't want that. Go away, I tell you..."

He put out his hand and rang the bell violently. Jean came running.

Paul stood up and, supporting himself on the furniture, headed for the sofa. He spoke, breathlessly: "Jean, my friend is at home here. Let no one try to see me, on any pretext, until tomorrow! But go away! I can; sleep until that accursed door is closed...and not to sleep would kill me...and kill her!"

It would have been cruel and imprudent to disobey him. I was witnessing a crisis whose immediate study was impossible for me. He had fallen on to the sofa and remained there, his eyes staring, as if dead, while his extended arm imperiously showed us the door.

We went out, and heard behind us the sound of bolts being violently shot.

I shall pass over the conversation that followed between Jean and me without delay. I had nothing to tell him and he brought no further elements to my appreciation of the situation. There was a foundation of peasant credulity in the worthy man, and if I had pressed him, it would not have taken much for him to attribute his master's condition to some evil spell. I ended up escaping from his chatter.

The house and the park being completely at my disposal, it was now a matter of spending my time in the best possible way. The inaction imposed upon me for twelve or fifteen hours seemed burdensome, but I judged that, in sum, I had made more progress than I had hoped the previous day. It was an important result to have been able to talk to Paul and to be certain that the conversation would be resumed on the following day.

There was no denying that I had found myself in a position of real inferiority in the conversation we had just had. Everything had surprised me: the words, the actions, the ideas. I was like a physician who sees a sick person for the first time, ignorant of his constitution and his antecedents, and who finds himself confounded by seemingly-contradictory morbid phenomena. It did not displease me to have time for reflection. I therefore tried to rid my mind of the shadows that were darkening it, and to formulate a plan for the next day's meeting.

It was necessary for me to forget that Paul was my friend, in order to be able to investigate at leisure, without my nerves getting in the way.

I took a long walk in the park on my own, taking an interest in its curious flora, born by virtue of dutiful care in a rocky terrain, as at the Château de Cintra, and in the course of those observations I gradually recovered the calmness of my consciousness and rationality.

Then, as a fine autumnal rain had begun to fall, I went back into the house. It comprised a ground floor and two upper floors; Paul's apartment was on the first, while I occupied the largest of the guest bedrooms on the second. On the ground floor there was a drawing-room whose windows looked out over the countryside, which was invisible in this grey weather. There was also a smoking-room, and a games room with a billiard table and a skittles table, all of which—I must do justice to Jean—was perfectly maintained in a state of exquisite neatness.

Finally, I found a little room, almost completely dark, with a leaded window: a library with shelves around the walls and an oak table in the middle. One immediately felt among friends. By the light of a lamp, I began examining the shelves, and discovered there—to my great satisfaction—the best of the most recent works of philosophy and the natural sciences. There was, however, also a collection of works relating to the strangest and murkiest problems of transcendent psychology, psychic studies and even—why recoil from the word?—magic, Oriental esotericism and full-blown occultism.

Ah! I said to myself. *This is what will probably give me the key to the mystery. These volumes are covered in notes, underlining and reminders; it's evident that Paul has read them repeatedly. It's necessary to have a very clear and well-equilibrated mind to lea over such depths without experiencing a sensation of vertigo and the void. Paul's head must have become dizzy. That's a curable affliction—a variety of neurosis with which suggestion can rapidly get to grips.*

I was reassured. Knowing the causes, I had less fear of the effects. Then as now, I was not an impenitent denier of mysterious phenomena, several of which—and not the least troubling—have already acquired the right to be cited in our clinics. I consider, however, that nothing is more dangerous than to set foot, like some fantastic tourist, on those unknown territories where madness is lying in wait for you. Paul was not armed for the struggle; the grief he had experienced had predisposed him to mental unsteadiness; he had stumbled carelessly at the first step. I would hold out my hand to him and help him up; it was my duty as a sane man and a friend, and I would not fail in it.

My anxiety lightened. I ate with a healthy appetite, cutting short Jean's dissertations. He gave me the impression of having submitted to the contagion of ambient derangement, and I retired to my room early, desirous of resting in order to be in full possession of my mental lucidity the following day.

I felt calm and I went to sleep without any fever. After a time that I could not measure, however, I suddenly awoke with a nervous hiccup—and, curiously enough, had exactly the same impression as the previous evening: an inexplicable anguish complicated by a bizarre difficulty in breathing.

I leapt on to the carpet, reacting with all my strength against that torpor. Either I was the victim of an illusion—in which case reason would dissipate it—or the phenomenon was real, and I would discover its cause.

I saw that the lamp, which I had left burning, was shining with a singular glare, as if the flame had been excited by an excessive supply of oxygen. A sharp odor of ether also seized my nostrils. It was these effluvia that were going to my head. The physical effect was so patent that for an instant my troubled sight seemed to perceive undulant and gyrating forms in the room.

I dressed hurriedly and opened my window. Their air did me good. The night was black, and there was not the slightest noise to be heard. I leaned out in order to breathe in the vivifying freshness more deeply, and by virtue of that movement I noticed that a window on the floor below was illuminated by a very soft whitish light; one might have thought that a cloud of infinitesimal dust particles was being exhaled therefrom.

Now, on examining the house more closely than I had previously done, I perceived that my own window opened on to a balcony that extended around a part of the story, and it occurred to me that from the most distant corner I might perhaps be able to see into the room that was so strangely lit—which, I now deduced, was adjacent to the room in which Paul had received me that morning. It was the eternally-closed study that Jean had mentioned.

Without disputing for a single instant my right to the indiscretion, I went out on to the balcony and, taking care to muffle the sound of my footsteps, followed the iron ramp in pitch darkness—certain, in consequence, of not being seen, even by the old domestic, if he were not yet asleep at this hour.

I thus arrived at the angle of the wing and found myself a few meters from the room in question, seeing it obliquely, but quite clearly. Interior curtains masked the greater part of it, but through a gap between them a light appeared, pale, or rather bluish, soft, and comparable— this was the thought that immediately sprang to mind— to that emitted by fireflies.

I leaned on my elbows, more emotional than I could have wished, with the light heartbeat familiar to naughty children. I could not deny that my curiosity was a trifle guilty.

For quite some time I did not observe anything more than that reflection of an invisible light-source, and I was thinking of going back to bed when I suddenly saw the curtain lifted up and....

Two shadows were outlined on the panes. I really mean two shadows, leaning toward one another, as if entwined.

And of those two silhouettes, I could only recognize one, which was that of my friend Paul. As for the other, there was no possibility of error: it was a female form, a slender Byzantine curve.

That apparition lasted as long as a flash of lightning before the curtain fell back.

However resistant my reason was, all objections fell before the fact: there was a woman in Paul's apartment, and I could swear, if my memory served me right—and I had the conviction that it was precise—that the slender silhouette, of mysterious, pre-Raphaelite design, was astonishingly similar to that of Virginie.

In any case, Jean was not mistaken. During the nights when access to his study was forbidden to everyone, Paul was not alone. At the same time, the hypothesis that I had previously rejected became compelling: Virginie living, a simulated death, by virtue of who knows what morbid caprice, and, finally, isolation *à deux*, in doubtless voluntary sequestration.

There was some macabre drama there that the madness of one, or perhaps both, was aggravating every day by prolonging it.

First light came; I felt cold. I went back into my room and slept until the morning.

X.

"Grant me two days," Paul said to me the following day, "and I'll reveal my secret to you."

I had not confessed the discovery I had made during the night, preferring to guide him to a more gradual confidence. To my great surprise, though, he undertook to answer my curiosity of his own accord.

He admitted, frankly, that his attitude must seem very strange, but he found himself in extraordinary circumstances, which authorized the most fantastic suppositions. Far from prohibiting them, he declared that I would remain, even so, short of the reality; the best thing was not to waste my time with futile hypotheses. If he could not give me immediate satisfaction, it was because he was not the sole master of his decisions; he had important interests to protect.

"There are modesties," he added, "which we other living beings cannot imagine!"

To be brief, I agreed to grant him the requested delay; after forty-eight hours he would be ready to initiate me into the mystery of his life.

The worst thing was that I had no idea of the nature of that mystery.

Examining him attentively, I was struck by the alteration of his physiognomy: his features were drawn, his eyes dark-ringed; even his voice had a strange, diminished timbre. Furthermore, he did not seek to hide an immense fatigue, and cut my visit short.

I had, of course, to promise not to try to see him during the two days of respite imposed upon me.

"To talk to you, listen to you, even to hear you would be a burden of fatigue that I do not have the right to take on. I need to concentrate, to synthesize all my energy, without any vain expense."

I agreed to everything, without any discussion, so fearful was I of saying something, in my ignorance, that might modify his resolution.

Dreading, however, that I might not be able to master my curiosity, further excited by the obscurity of his promises, I declared that I would absent myself for those two days, promising to be ready, sat the appointed hour, to take advantage of his good will.

"Will you give me your word," I said to him, "that you won't commit any imprudence?"

"None," he said, with a smile. "In your turn, I want to give you some advice…"

"What?"

"In order that the transition between the known and…the unknown might be less abrupt for you, it's necessary that I ask you during this delay to make every effort to combat the old skepticism that, in spite of your open mind, is still ready to reappear. Meditate upon the fine words of Arago: *Outside pure mathematics, the word impossible has no meaning.*"

"That's my opinion too," I replied, shaking his hand. "I'm damned if I don't believe in the supernatural a little already." Privately, I was alluding to the strangeness of the night.

He shrugged his shoulders. "Don't employ words without meaning, then. There's no such thing as the supernatural. Electricity appears supernatural to a savage, and the phonograph to an Academician. There are only changes of plane and perspective—but don't draw me into discussion; it's a waste of energy."

Jean was disappointed to see me go. He imagined that I was abandoning his master to madness and possession; he believed, naively, that demonic activity as at work. I did my best to reassure him, and left.

I returned to Paris, and, in truth, breathed more freely. The atmosphere of Pierre-Sèche had contracted my lungs in some way, and it was with delight that I lived those forty-eight hours of normal existence. The thought even occurred to me that if I had to spend any considerable time out there, if only to attempt to cure my friend's mental illness, I ought to take a supply of Parisian air.

I bought items in vogue, including the most fashionable novels, and took out subscriptions to current periodicals. I begged a friend to write to me often and keep me up to date with the thousand incidents of everyday life—in brief, not knowing exactly what the future had in store for me in that bizarre house, I took precautions to combat the threatened hauntings. In addition, the most recent scientific works would bring me back to my favorite studies. I was forearmed, like a ferry-passenger who anticipates a difficult crossing.

Equipped with my intellectual provisions, with which I had created considerable scope for distractions of the imagination, I made my way back to Salbris.

I arrived at the castle before the appointed hour; that was intentional. I wanted to have time to arrange my books, to have them close to hand in case of need. Jean was waiting for me at the gate in a state of excitement that frightened me at first, but it was nothing very serious. For twenty-four hours, Paul had not opened his door. Jean had listened, spied—what frightened him the most was that he had not discovered anything.

But Paul was alive; that was the only thing he had ascertained, and the one that was most important to me. I was there now, with a perfectly sane mind, utterly determined to triumph over any monomania whatsoever.

We transported my boxes to the library, and the books of occult science with which the shelves were garnished must have quivered with anger, forced as they were to squeeze together to make way for the works of healthy reason and carefully-weighed imagination. Having done that, I consulted my watch, which marked precisely six o'clock. Paul's bell rang. Jean went up.

I was slightly fearful that Paul would ask for a further delay, but I did not have to dispense a further dose of patience. Paul was waiting for me. I went up to his room rapidly.

He received me very gladly. I even had the satisfaction of seeing that he seemed no weaker than before my departure.

"Well," I said, merrily, "you see that I'm on time; for your part, you seem disposed to keep your promise. Here I am, my ears and mind open, ready to listen to your fairy tale."

"Don't take that light tone," he replied, "for never in our lives—never you hear—has there been a more serious moment."

I held out my hand; he clasped it with his own.

"Admit," he said, "that you think I'm mad."

"I swear to you…"

"Don't swear, for there was also a time when I thought that my reason had abandoned me, and you will understand that later when you appreciate that it requires strength to remain master of one's brain when, in response to a breath of wind from who knows where, the profound portal to the unknown slowly opens."

His voice had trembled slightly; I was more disturbed than I wanted to appear.

"I assure you," I went on, determinedly, "that you will not encounter any prejudice in me, nor any fixed notion, nor any irony in poor taste. Speak to me, therefore, in total confidence. I have always loved you, and we have worked through the most arduous problems together. Whatever terrain you might draw me into, you will find me standing firm upon it, and in good faith. I'm listening."

He thanked me with a grateful smile. I had told the truth. I find all negation *a priori* ridiculous.

He leaned forward hen, with his head in his hands, and for a minute, I had to wonder whether he was still mindful of the fact that I was there—but he raised his head again and looked me in the face. Then, reaching out to a crystal decanter half-full of a golden chartreuse, he placed it directly in the light and said: "Look at this attentively—with all eyes, as they say—with a firm desire to remember its form and its color. Don't speak, don't think—look!"

Gripped by an interest that I was unable to deny, and also, I must confess, dominated by the authority of his manner and his voice, I concentrated all my visual attention on the decanter that he was showing me.

It was made of a very pure crystal, with a few delicate carving around the neck in the form of elongated olives. The main body of the decanter was nicely rounded, and toward the bottom other olivettes extended to the base.

The liqueur, entirely golden, was vibrating round a sunlit dot that was almost dazzling.

All that I saw within a second, with an acuity of detailed attention that I had never known before.

"Now close your eyes," he instructed me, in the same abrupt tone, with which I immediately complied.

"Once again, look, inside yourself, at the decanter. Can't you see it?"

"I can see it!" I exclaimed.

For a time that I cannot specify, I saw the decanter as clearly as if my eyes had been open: the contours of the crystal, the sparkling of the liqueur. I wanted to retain that image, that internal photograph—but everything faded away."

"Bah!" I said, reopening my eyes. "It's the well-known phenomenon of visual memory."

He made a gesture of impatience and exclaimed: "Visual memory! Ah, that's your scientific method, words responding to words! What is memory? You don't know, but you've named, labeled a faculty; you've categorized it and catalogued it in your dictionary—and you're satisfied! Moreover, it's necessary that everyone does likewise, under pain of anathema. Come on, speak—answer me in all sincerity! What is memory? How does it work? What is its organ? Oh yes, an image forms on the retina, is transmitted by a network of nerves to your brain…by what mechanism?"

I could see that he as excited; I wanted to calm him down.

"Note that I'm not formulating any theory; I'm not an adversary, but a friend—perhaps very ignorant, but, at any rate, full of good will…"

"You promised not to employ irony. Well, yes, I shall instruct you in spite of yourself…and here's my formula: visual memory is the projection outside ourselves of a form stored within us."

"The definition is not disagreeable to me…"

"I call your attention to the projection that I shall call physical, that of the form, of the exterior shell of things. When you think about a book, you see its form more-or-less clearly…"

"That's true."

"If you remember a horse, you have before your eyes the more-or-less correct outline of the animal…"

"That's right again."

"Well, suppose that you exercise your will to improve, to accentuate that outline—as a painter does, for example. You project your memory outside yourself, and you make use of it as an adequate model, all proportions retained, as a living model that is set before your eyes…"

"I don't deny…"

"Then imagine that you are concentrating your volitional energy increasingly in the sense of that improvement and accentuation. Increase the force of contemplation, increase your faculty of mental restitution, now exterior, and you will gradually succeed in creating what I will still only call the illusion of the real existence of the remembered object. But the truth is that it is not an illusion but a reality. That form that you have absorbed by your attention, which you possess within you, you really project externally. It exists, you hear; it is—this is the truth—a *restitution* of infinitesimal material particles that you have appropriated in looking at the object, aspired by virtue of your attention and stored within yourself. That reconstitution is no illusion, but an existent entity; it is…"

I interrupted him. "In my turn, let me tell you that there is nothing here but hypotheses, which, ingenious as they are, need to be supported by proofs…"

He did not let me finish. "Abandon your methods of university sophistry, then. Why should the form that you see outside yourself be any less existent whether it is produced by the banal fact of presence or by what you call the imagination?"

"Because I can touch the one and not the other, and thus establish the existence of the reality."

I had pronounced these last words sharply—and, admittedly, a trifle harshly.

"What if I prove to you that you can touch…your illusion?" he exclaimed. "Have you ever possessed the memory of a form imprinted so profoundly in your soul that it is real and alive there, and that you are able to project it outside yourself, as it is within you, with all the attributes of reality and life? Oh, it is necessary to love, to have loved; it's necessary to have aspired, resorbed, inhaled all the effluvia of the adored individual, for there to remain within you…so that then, at the beginning of solitude, closing your eyes, you can see her again in her radiant and perfect reality…

"But is that all? No! Succeed in drowning yourself in that unique desire, that immense determination to communicate to that form all the energy and vital force that you have…and then you will reconstitute her, that being of your soul, blood of your blood, flesh of your flesh, substance of your substance, living, resuscitated and recreated, as Aischa, Eve, was evoked from the Paradisal Adam, under the sublime light of the eternal spheres!"

"Take care, my friend!" I cried. "This excitement is killing you!"

"Not at all—it's my life! Oh, you were able to believe that my Virginie was dead, and that I, egotistical or insane, had the shameful courage to survive her! No, no, she is not dead. I have her…she is alive in me, here, in my heart, in my breast, in my brain. She is alive; I see her adorable and smiling, and, like a sensitive bird that sleeps in my being, I can, when I wish, open the door of her cage for her…

"Come, come—you shall see her, you also—for she is going to emerge from my heart!"

XI.

He had grabbed me by the hand, dragging me away. I did not resist, reckoning that in crises of that sort, contradiction is both futile and perilous.

We had arrived at the door to the study, always closed until then. Setting his fingers on the key, he said, in a low voice, with extreme volubility: "Listen—for you, but for you alone, I will commit a sacrilege; I will violate the sublime secret, but She has permitted it. Above all, don't say a word. Hold your breath, and watch."

We had entered into complete darkness. Outside, the night was now profound; no glimmer of light filtered through the thick curtains. His eyes had doubtless become accustomed to that darkness over a long period, for he led me without hesitation to the far side of the room, and pushed me into an armchair.

Is it surprising that I was seized by a profound anguish? It was the emotion that Latins called *horror*, which gripped the heart of the neophyte at the threshold of the sacred wood.

I dared not make a movement; with my upper body thrust forward, and my head feverish, I waited in an agony of anxiety.

I could not see Paul, but I gradually perceived the increasing sound of his respiration—or, rather, long sighs, which stopped abruptly for several seconds after concluding in a profound expiration.

I could not take accurate account of time, but those pauses seemed interminable…

Then, from a certain point within the room—I soon saw that Paul was there, on a sofa—a white light expanded, which seemed to me to be reminiscent of exceedingly thin cigar smoke. That mist condensed into a vaguely agitated thread, tending to rise up. Then it broadened out and extended, still rising in a powerful jet. It was rotating very slowly, now multiplied by other puffs of mist, which melted into it, forming a cloud whose particles seemed animated by a movement of vertiginous intensity.

From this whirlwind of molecules a feeble light emerged—which was, however, sufficient for me to see my friend in the aforementioned location, his head lying on a cushion and his eyes shut, as if he were asleep. He was so pale! A lunar whiteness!

The mist condensed; the gyration agitating it slowed down; it became, so to speak, fixed—and, little by little, a form became more precise, contours more clearly delineated. It became an image, at first very vague, like an extremely faded pastel drawing.

As the precision became more accentuated, deeper sighs—almost groans—escaped Paul's lungs, and the ever-more-distinct form, which was obviously a woman, undulated in strict unison with his inspirations and expirations. At each of his movements it took on more solidity, as if—if I might put it thus—that breath were a vital nutriment.

Between the two of them ran a thread of vapor, which appeared to be rooted in the sleeper's breast.

And it was then that I understood what he had tried to explain. She was born of his heart!

Yes, it really was his heart that was exhaling and exteriorizing that form, which took on a vitality…and, spectral at first, was gradually clad in all the appearances—should I say appearances?—of life.

Was I mad myself when I now recognized Virginie, the pure and dear child: not a phantom more sinister than the corpse itself, but an individual possessed of a gaze, who was breathing, who had all the attributes of existence? No, I cannot lie to myself; it was really her, resuscitated, returned from the world from which—it is believed—no one can ever return: the adored Virginie, revivified by love.

Yes, a miracle of love in all its power; she lived again by virtue of the man who had conserved her within him and who, by the sublime gift of himself, restored, animated and vitalized the beloved creature that he carried, still living, within himself.

His eyes were now wide open, and they were fixed on her eyes—those eyes whose bluish tints, with wisps of burnished silver, I recognized.

I was half-standing, desirous of approaching but not daring to do so.

He gestured to me, and I understood that he was summoning me; he pointed to a decanter that was on a side-table. I took hold of it and opened it. The ethylic perfume of ether spread forth, and I observed, to my great surprise, that in response to the effluvia of the odorant substance, the apparent vitality of the phantom became even more evident.

The young woman was kneeling next to Paul, and her hands were clasping his. Were they speaking? I could not hear any words, and yet I divined that they were saying exquisite things, silently.

How was it that I found myself kneeling beside them, and that Paul, smiling, put my hand in Virginie's? She looked at me with the understanding expression that is the renewal of old friendships, and I felt her supple little fingers within my hand, responding to my discreet embrace.

I placed my hand on her heart—Paul had doubtless authorized me to do so—and that heart was beating.

XII.

For a month I lived in that world of dreams, without even trying to remove myself from the envelopment that circumscribed me more narrowly every day. Mystery is a narcotic, a sphinx both hypnotic and intoxicating.

Finally, one day, I awoke from that torpor. Come on! Was I, like so many others—like Bulwer's Zanoni—to allow myself to be vanquished by the Dweller of the Threshold?[41] Paralyzed and broken, was I going to forget the obligations of real life, to become perpetually drunk on the absinthe of the beyond? Had I the right to betray myself, to deliver myself bound hand and foot to the imbecile inebriety of the occult? Was this unhealthy delight in disequilibration worth as much as the normal satisfactions that forceful scientific study provides?

I had witnessed amazing and most unexpected phenomena, but why, after all, should they trouble me more than the astonishing experiments carried out a hundred

---

[41] The occult revival was considerably boosted by the enormous popularity of Edward Bulwer-Lytton's neo-Rosicrucian fantasy *Zanoni* (1842), which was greatly admired and to some extent plagiarized by both "Eliphas Lévi" and Madame Blavatsky. In the novel, the would-be initiate into occult mysteries, Glyndon, abandons his ambitions after his confrontation with the dire Dweller of the Threshold, but Zanoni, who has already met that initial challenge successfully, makes a deal with the Dweller in the hope of saving his wife and child from death—which, like most quasi-diabolical pacts, goes sadly awry. It is significant, in the context of the present story, that the self-deceiving narrator refers to Zanoni's "vanquishment" rather than Glyndon's intimidation.

times over in the laboratory? It was, I conceded, an opening to a new world, but why hypnotize oneself before a door opened by a crack? Was it not, on the contrary, necessary to polish up all one's scientific instruments, in order to penetrate the unknown better armed, and seize the secret by the throat?

The supernatural does not exist...there are merely changes of plane. The first man who made fire did not remain petrified before a conflagration that was incomprehensible to him; he learned its uses, and made himself master of it.

I too would make myself master of the occult, but without the impatience that disturbs reason and disorganizes effort. I would begin by learning more about that which was normal, after which I would push on to that which still seemed abnormal.

When these thoughts imposed themselves upon me, thanks to a reaction of my consciousness, I experienced the ineffable joy of a swimmer in peril who feels solid ground beneath his feet. I too was resuscitated; I became myself again; I freed myself from an enervating haunting.

At the same time, though, I understood that my task must not be purely egotistical. By absorbing himself in the contemplation of the unknown, my friend was obviously heading toward madness. Even assuming that his strength could resist a quotidian hyperexcitation, and assuming that the over-extended springs of his mind would not snap in a mortal catastrophe, it was certain that his absorption by his obsession would lead to a sentimental monomania, to the point of a decisive accident of cerebral disaggregation.

Curiously enough, I probably owed to that excursion to the limit of alienation a more unassailable firmness of reason, and also a more irreducible tenacity of will.

I set myself a double mission.

I had no great difficulty in accomplishing the first part: scarcely a week had gone by since I made my resolution than I witnessed with the most perfect self-composure a new phenomenon of exteriorization. I had killed any excessive curiosity within me, even the desire to lift the veil that still covered the genesis of the mystery. I knew that a day would come when my studies, logically conducted, would guide me to the solution of the problem.

The second objective was more difficult to attain. As you will have guessed, I wanted to cure my friend, to snatch him back from the beyond, from his illusions—yes, illusions, since he and he alone could give life to an appearance, to an empty shell. I wanted to bring him back to reality.

Fortunately, I was sufficiently master of myself not to deviate from the plan that I had drawn up on the first day, and whose first stage could be described thus: the division of his attention.

We were no longer apart. Old Jean looked at me with a harrowing expression, thinking that I was as mad as his master. I did not think it advisable to disabuse him, fearing an intervention on his part that would have compromised everything.

As I made no attempt to deny the reality of the apparition, and accepted Paul's mystical theories without contradiction, there came a time when we had exhausted that subject of conversation. It was then that I talked to him about my own studies. I had organized a chemistry laboratory in the cellars of the little château, and I had adopted as a theme the genesis of the elements, according to the theories of William Crookes.[42]

This work impassioned me to such a degree that I soon felt that I was endowed with the strength necessary to impose my influence on my friend. During the few hours he had to spare each day I had first to wake him up, then develop and excite his scientific curiosity, in order that he might become a zealous collaborator.

Oh, I sometimes asked myself if I were not doing a bad, almost cowardly, deed since my adversary...it was Her, the beloved that I wanted to get rid of, the intruder that I wanted to send away...to the tomb of silence and immobility!

One day, during a marvelous experiment in the spectral analysis of the primary metals, I achieved the unprecedented result that Paul forgot the usual hour of his macabre rendezvous. He let more than fifty minutes pass thus. When he noticed it he had a veritable fit of despair, almost of rage. I calmed him down as best I could and went with him—but he had expended such a sum of attention in following the changes of the prism that he had infinite difficulty in evoking the expected image—and such was the effort that, just as I was really beginning to conceive great anxieties regarding the out-

---

[42] Crookes' experiments in spectroscopy, which allowed him to distinguish several elements that were difficult to discriminate in terms of their chemical behavior, and helped to lay the final groundwork for the periodic table of the elements, led him to develop the hypothesis that the elements had formed by a process akin to polymerization when a superheated "primal matter" cooled. He proposed it in an address to the British Association for the Advancement of Science in September 1886, and it generated several responses in 1887, but it was virtually forgotten thereafter.

come of the séance, the springs of his energy relaxed and he slipped into a profound sleep.

As is understandable, I experienced the greatest difficulty in renewing my treason. I had to give him my word of honor that I would never permit him to forget the hour of his funereal rendezvous again.

As I studied him further, however, my Machiavellianism found new means of operation. I gradually succeeded in interesting him not merely in the arid sciences, but also in the contemporary movement of ideas. Although he fought shy of it at first, the demon of investigation and debate took hold of him. I provoked his contradictions myself, and that cerebral effort resulted in a diminution of effort that reduced the clarity of the apparition.

I rarely witnessed that evocation, which was always the same, save only with less precision.

For several days I saw him become sadder, more absorbed than usual. I dared not interrogate him, being all too aware of my partial responsibility for his melancholy.

He refused all conversation, shutting himself away in his room and bolting the door. I knew that he was cloistering himself in the study early. The flasks of ether were emptying rapidly. He no longer asked me to accompany him, but I kept watch without him being aware of it; I had even procured duplicate keys to his bedroom and study. While he devoted himself to his dolorous experiments, I stayed on the other side of the door, my ear stuck to the panel, in a state of indescribable anguish.

One evening, when he had shut himself in for more than two hour, I heard a heart-rending cry, like a death-rattle, and, at the same time, the sound of a fall. Within a second, I was beside him. He was lying on the floor in the middle of the study, prey to epileptic convulsions. I lifted him up and carried him in my arms out of the ether-saturated atmosphere. He was livid, with a deathly expression.

I succeeded in bringing him round—but then he sat up straight, his features contracted, crying: "She doesn't love me any more...she's abandoning me...Virginie, Virginie, why haven't you come?"

Then there was a crisis, which resembled a fit of furious madness.

The next day, Paul was gripped by an intense fever, complicated by an acute delirium.

I summoned a friend by telegraph—a great physician from Paris—who came immediately, and I told him everything.

He had the audacity to make a violent resolution. Whatever the risk, it was necessary to remove Paul from the environment that maintained is dolorous passion. It was certain that if he remained at Pierre-Sèche, the haunting would take possession of him again at the slightest flash of reason, and the tension of his will, exercised on weary organs, would lead infallibly to his death.

"Let's take him to my house in Paris," said the great physician. "It's necessary to abolish his memory of the past."

I obeyed. It was a sad pilgrimage, but the cerebral commotion had been too great for the invalid to take account of what was happening. We were able to remove him from Pierre-Sèche and install him in the doctor's apartment without his even being aware of any displacement.

For more than three months, we despaired of saving him. We were admirably supported in our task by the doctor's sister, an intelligent and pretty young widow whose premature misfortune had made her compassionate to the suffering of others. She was overwhelmed by a sympathy for the young fellow who now seemed to have no more will-power than a child and who, in the first phase of his convalescence, experienced infinite joy in finding himself alive.

Naturally, I had kept old Jean away, and I stayed out of sight myself as much as possible, wanting his intelligence to reawaken in an entirely new environment.

Dare I say that I had had the audacity to reveal all to my colleague's sister, explaining to her that Paul had nearly died of regret for a dead woman, and that he might perhaps live...by virtue of being loved by a living one.

One never addresses oneself in vain to the pity of women; besides, did that one not love him already, by virtue of all the devotion she had lavished upon him—the long hours spent to is bedside, the cups pressed to his lips, the gentle reprimands that even the most patient nurse cannot avoid?

As for me, if it was a sacrilege to send Virginie back to her tomb, I committed it in total clarity of conscience.

It was on a gracious female face, healthy and young, with a glint of mischief in her eyes, that Paul's eyes first rested. The charm with which she enveloped him, with the heroism of merciful coquetry, impeded and delayed the awakening of his memory.

I reappeared at his beside myself, and he seemed surprised to see me. Our intimacy was renewed. No allusion was made to events at Pierre-Sèche. I sometimes sensed that he wanted to question me, but I also understood that his memories were sufficiently vague for him to doubt their reality.

Aided by the woman, I guided his re-entry to reality step by step; without constraint, I steered his ideas in the direction of the practical and normal; I interested him in actualities, enough for him to have no need for recourse to the intellectual aliment of memory. To be completely honest, though, my most powerful auxiliary was the love—built on gratitude and submission—that he consecrated to the woman who had saved him.

It was only after six months of convalescence, when his strength had been completely restored, that he ventured to question me about the past.

He would have said that I had committed all sorts of moral crimes. I lied boldly, explaining to him that since the death of his first wife he had been in a state of intellectual health that sometimes had the appearance of hallucination. He dared not press me too hard, but I had the audacity to reply to his most secret thoughts by telling him that, in fits of delirium, he thought he had seen the person he had lost.

Fortunately, his weakened brain was no longer able to reconstruct the chains of abstruse reasoning necessary to mystical conceptions. He believed me, by virtue of lassitude—and because he wanted to believe me, and free himself from his past.

And thus it was that poor Virginie—I have the hypocrisy to lament!—died for a second time, never to be evoked again: an image forever effaced, borne away by the eternal reflux of the sea of forgetfulness, according to the ineluctable and benevolent law that regulates people and things.

SF & FANTASY

Guy d'Armen. *Doc Ardan: The City of Gold and Lepers*
G.-J. Arnaud. *The Ice Company*
Aloysius Bertrand. *Gaspard de la Nuit*
Félix Bodin. *The Novel of the Future*
Didier de Chousy. *Ignis*
C. I. Defontenay. *Star (Psi Cassiopeia)*
Charles Derennes. *The People of the Pole*
Harry Dickson. *The Heir of Dracula*
 Sâr Dubnotal *vs. Jack the Ripper*
Alexandre Dumas. *The Return of Lord Ruthven*
J.-C. Dunyach. *The Night Orchid. The Thieves of Silence*
Paul Féval. *Anne of the Isles. Knightshade. Revenants. Vampire City. The Vampire Countess. The Wandering Jew's Daughter*
Paul Féval, *fils. Felifax, the Tiger-Man*
Arnould Galopin. *Doctor Omega*
V. Hugo, Foucher & Meurice. *The Hunchback of Notre-Dame*
O. Joncquel & Theo Varlet. *The Martian Epic*
Jean de La Hire. *Enter the Nyctalope. The Nyctalope on Mars. The Nyctalope vs. Lucifer*
G. Le Faure & H. de Graffigny. *The Extraordinary Adventures of a Russian Scientist Across the Solar System* (2 vols.)
Gustave Le Rouge. *The Vampires of Mars*
Jules Lermina. *Panic in Paris. To-Ho and the Gold Destroyers. Mysteryville*
Jean-Marc & Randy Lofficier. *Edgar Allan Poe on Mars. The Katrina Protocol. Pacifica. Robonocchio.* (anthologists) *Tales of the Shadowmen* (6 vols.) (non-fiction) *Shadowmen* (2 vols.)
Xavier Mauméjean. *The League of Heroes*
Marie Nizet. *Captain Vampire*
C. Nodier, Beraud & Toussaint-Merle. *Frankenstein*
Henri de Parville. *An Inhabitant of the Planet Mars*
Polidori, C. Nodier, E. Scribe. *Lord Ruthven the Vampire*
P.-A. Ponson du Terrail. *The Vampire and the Devil's Son*

Maurice Renard. *Doctor Lerne. A Man Among the Microbes. The Blue Peril*

Albert Robida. *The Clock of the Centuries. The Adventures of Saturnin Farandoul*

J.-H. Rosny Aîné. *The Navigators of Space. The World of the Variants*

Brian Stableford. *The Shadow of Frankenstein. Frankenstein and the Vampire Countess. The New Faust at the Tragicomique. Sherlock Holmes & The Vampires of Eternity. The Stones of Camelot. The Wayward Muse.* (anthologist) *The Germans on Venus. News from the Moon*

Kurt Steiner. *Ortog*

Villiers de l'Isle-Adam. *The Scaffold. The Vampire Soul*

Philippe Ward. *Artahe*

MYSTERIES & THRILLERS

M. Allain & P. Souvestre. *The Daughter of Fantômas*

Anicet-Bourgeois, Lucien Dabril. *Rocambole*

A. Bisson & G. Livet. *Nick Carter vs. Fantômas*

V. Darlay & H. de Gorsse. *Lupin vs. Holmes: The Stage Play*

Paul Féval. *The Black Coats: The Companions of the Treasure. Gentlemen of the Night. Heart of Steel. The Invisible Weapon. John Devil. The Parisian Jungle. 'Salem Street*

Emile Gaboriau. *Monsieur Lecoq*

Steve Leadley. *Sherlock Holmes: The Circle of Blood*

Maurice Leblanc. *Arsène Lupin: The Hollow Needle. The Blonde Phantom*

Gaston Leroux. *Chéri-Bibi. The Phantom of the Opera. Rouletabille & the Mystery of the Yellow Room*

G. Marot & L. Pericaud. *Nick Carter vs. Jack the Ripper*

William Patrick Maynard. *The Terror of Fu Manchu*

Frank J. Morlock. *Sherlock Holmes: The Grand Horizontals*

P. de Wattyne & Y. Walter. *Sherlock Holmes vs. Fantômas*

David White. *Fantômas in America*